THE
RESURRECTION
TABLET

A James Acton Thriller

Also by J. Robert Kennedy

James Acton Thrillers

The Protocol
Brass Monkey
Broken Dove
The Templar's Relic
Flags of Sin
The Arab Fall
The Circle of Eight
The Venice Code
Pompeii's Ghosts
Amazon Burning
The Riddle

Blood Relics
Sins of the Titanic
Saint Peter's Soldiers
The Thirteenth Legion
Raging Sun
Wages of Sin
Wrath of the Gods
The Templar's Revenge
The Nazi's Engineer
Atlantis Lost
The Cylon Curse
The Viking Deception

Keepers of the Lost Ark
The Tomb of Genghis Khan
The Manila Deception
The Fourth Bible
Embassy of the Empire
Armageddon
No Good Deed
The Last Soviet
Lake of Bones
Fatal Reunion
The Resurrection Tablet

Special Agent Dylan Kane Thrillers

Rogue Operator
Containment Failure
Cold Warriors
Death to America

Black Widow
The Agenda
Retribution

State Sanctioned
Extraordinary Rendition
Red Eagle
The Messenger

Templar Detective Thrillers

The Templar Detective
The Parisian Adulteress

The Sergeant's Secret
The Unholy Exorcist
The Code Breaker

The Black Scourge
The Lost Children

Kriminalinspektor Wolfgang Vogel Mysteries

The Colonel's Wife

Sins of the Child

Delta Force Unleashed Thrillers

Payback
Infidels
The Lazarus Moment

Kill Chain
Forgotten

The Cuban Incident
Rampage
Inside the Wire

Detective Shakespeare Mysteries

Depraved Difference

Tick Tock

The Redeemer

Zander Varga, Vampire Detective

The Turned

THE RESURRECTION TABLET

A James Acton Thriller

J. ROBERT KENNEDY

UnderMill
PRESS

Copyright ©2022 J. Robert Kennedy

ISBN: 9781990418334

First Edition

For my daughter, who came through for me when I needed her most.

THE RESURRECTION TABLET

A James Acton Thriller

"When he arose, his eyes were drenched with blood, a pathetic and pitiable sight that made everyone who saw it cry uncontrollably."

Michael Attaleiates
Official Roman Chronicler, c. AD 1072

"Now upon the first day of the week, very early in the morning, they came unto the sepulcher, bringing the spices which they had prepared, and certain others with them. And they found the stone rolled away from the sepulcher. And they entered in, and found not the body of the Lord Jesus."

Luke 24:1-3
King James Version

PREFACE

Those with at least a casual familiarity of history will have heard of the Byzantine Empire, or Byzantium. All but the most closeted will have heard of the Roman Empire. What many don't realize is that they are two halves of the same whole, and that if one were to travel back in time and meet a Byzantine citizen, they would have never heard the term, and would refer to themselves as Roman, or Romanian.

At its peak, the Roman Empire was simply too vast to effectively rule solely from Rome, and in AD 330, with the troubles in western and northern Europe, Emperor Constantine moved the capital of the empire from Rome to Constantinople, the renamed and rebuilt city of Byzantium. Over the years, the empire effectively split into the Western Roman Empire, ruled from Rome, and the Eastern Roman Empire, ruled from Constantinople.

By the late fifth century, the power and influence of the Western Roman Empire was negligible, and it faded into insignificance then oblivion. Yet the Eastern Roman Empire thrived for another thousand years. Constantinople was the most populous city in Europe for centuries, was the center of arts and culture, and contained the largest cathedral ever constructed for over 1000 years. But as most empires do, it eventually began its own decline.

One man tried to change all that, to save the empire he loved, by becoming emperor in a most unusual way. His first attempt was traditional, but his coup failed. Yet he still managed to become emperor without a single sword drawn.

Ultimately, he failed to save the empire he loved, abandoning his prudence in battle and instead making reckless decisions that made little sense at the time. For what those except his most trusted advisor didn't know, was that he had made a monumental discovery that could destroy the very foundations of the empire, and rock the world a millennium later.

The Resurrection Tablet.

Istanbul, Turkey
Present Day, Three Weeks From Now

"It should be directly ahead."

Retired Lt. Colonel Cameron Leather, former British Special Air Service, readied his illegal weapon. They were in Turkey, and none of his men were licensed to carry here, but this might be their only chance to rescue their client, Archaeology Professor James Acton. The man had been held captive for hours now, but their CIA contacts had located him and it had been decided they had to act.

Their local contact, Vasif Irmak, driving their SUV to the scene, had provided them with weapons, the man an old friend who understood how the world really worked, though none of them were sure what was going on here today.

Acton had just committed several crimes, including assault and theft, and was wanted by the Turkish authorities for acts of terrorism. If Leather's team didn't rescue the man before the police found him, he'd be dead in a shootout. They needed to retrieve him and get him either

3

out of the country, or safely into the hands of the authorities with a believable explanation for his actions today.

"On your right, twenty meters."

Leather readied himself as they slowed. "You're sure he's still inside?" he asked the voice over the speaker.

"Negative. We have footage of him entering, but there could be other ways out that aren't covered."

"Understood." He spotted something. "Stand by." He pointed at two men emerging from the restaurant. "They look like our guys, don't they?"

"Affirmative," said one of his men. "It looks like they might be getting ready to leave."

An SUV pulled up and the men opened the doors on the passenger side. Three more men from inside the café stepped into the sunlight and Leather recognized Acton right away.

"I've got eyes on the target. Moving to intercept."

Irmak hammered on the gas and surged past the SUV, cutting it off as they all jumped out. But it was too late. As they approached, they were spotted and Acton had been shoved into the back seat, the others jumping in after him. The SUV backed up then angled around them, the rear window rolling down as it passed. Acton leaned out and Leather sprinted toward him to pull him free, but instead a gun appeared and Acton opened fire.

Emptying the mag at those who were supposed to protect him.

What the hell is going on?

Great Palace of Constantinople

Constantinople, Eastern Roman Empire

AD 1067

This wasn't supposed to be her life. Eudokia Makrembolitissa had married a powerful man from an even more powerful family with the full knowledge he could become emperor of Rome. It meant she would become empress. She had no problem with that, and in fact, had enjoyed it immensely. The power and prestige of being the woman behind the man who ran the most powerful empire in the world was intoxicating, and when her husband, Constantine X was alive, life had been good.

In fact, it had been fantastic.

But he was dead, and on his deathbed, she had sworn to never remarry. Her reason was partly for love—she couldn't imagine giving her heart to another man, though it was also for their sons, specifically Michael, too young yet to rule. Co-regents had been appointed, yet they were fools, and she had managed to push them aside.

She was *Megalē Basilis tōn Romaiōn*, the Great Empress of Rome, or so said the coins she had ordered minted with her likeness and that of her two sons. No one could doubt her power, though many could not abide by the idea that a woman now led the Roman Empire. In fact, it enraged many.

While she usually didn't concern herself with men's egos, today she was forced to. Before the Senate stood Romanus Diogenes, son of Constantine Diogenes, and a thorn in her side. His family was from Cappadocia, both powerful and wealthy, and his relations included the blood of previous emperors.

He was a force to be reckoned with. A military commander of note, today he was being tried for an attempted coup—he had failed to overthrow the rightful rulers of the empire.

Her sons.

"Do you deny the charges?" asked one of the senators, whom, she didn't care. They were of no consequence to her. An emperor or empress humored the Senate—should she wish it, she could order them all killed and replaced with sheep. Yet all leaders tolerated them, for they could serve a purpose.

Romanus, in full dress, every bit the Roman soldier, stood proud and addressed the man. "I deny nothing. The actions I undertook were for the good of the empire, not for personal profit or gain."

Eudokia leaned on the arm of her throne, taking in the man, his booming voice demanding attention. He exuded confidence, despite facing certain death—no one attempted to take over the throne and lived. He was a handsome man, in fact, he was stunning. His body, much of it revealed by the armor he wore, exposed muscles that rippled with every thrust of his arm as he spoke, his words lost on her.

He could be the solution to her problem.

"You expect us to believe that?"

"I care not what you believe. The empire has grown weak and its enemies are at its gates. City after city is sacked, and we do nothing about it. The empire is vulnerable, its armies a shadow of their former selves, its citizens begging for someone to protect them, to restore the glory that was once Rome. Rome fell centuries ago from the same complacency. The barbarians threatened our gates and we gave in, ceding a little more territory each time, until finally they were no longer at our figurative gates, but our literal gates. They broke down the gates of Rome, swarmed her streets, slaughtered her citizens, and now Constantinople is all that stands. We have built a city as great as Rome, greater even, and have brought peace and stability to our lands.

"Yet the barbarians are once again at our gates. This time it isn't the Germanic tribes from the north, but the Turks and the Muslims. They want what we have, and we sit back and give it to them. It is time for a military ruler to take over, rebuild our armies and defeat our enemies, lest what happened to Rome happen to Constantinople. This is why I did what I did, not for the glory of one man, but for the glory of the empire, and its thousand-year history."

Someone clapped, a single smack of the hands ringing out before whoever delivered it thought better of it and sat on his hands. But she didn't care. Her mind raced at his words, for he was right. The armies had been left to wither over the centuries, with the empire now relying far too heavily on mercenaries whose loyalties went to the highest bidder. Romanus was correct in that the armies needed to be rebuilt, and their enemies taught a lesson. Yet she couldn't do that. Not on her own. And her sons were no warriors, too young to command the respect of not only the soldiers under their command, but their enemies.

But a man such as this would command that respect. He could lead armies of men who would rally to his cry, he could strike fear into the heart of their enemy and defeat them on the battlefield. He was the solution to the empire's problem, which meant he was the solution to her problem, for if she didn't solve this soon, the next coup attempt might just succeed.

Yet she couldn't simply hand the man power. Power had to remain in her hands, and those of her sons. There was only one solution she could think of, and it would require many to be convinced after the vow she had made.

"Romanus Diogenes, you are hereby found guilty of treason and attempting to usurp the throne from its rightful heirs. You will be held in chains until the Empress confirms your sentence, which can only be death."

Romanus remained silent, his jaw squared as he took the news as only a brave soldier could—with dignity. There was no pleading for his life, no begging for forgiveness. He reacted exactly as a leader should. If captured on the battlefield, and threatened with torture or execution, he would act the same, she was certain. He would die bravely, setting an example for those who followed him, perhaps rallying them to his banner with his death, ultimately bringing his army victory.

And his death now could lead to the same thing, turning him into a martyr to be rallied behind, encouraging more attempts to overthrow her and her sons.

It couldn't be tolerated.

It wouldn't be tolerated.

She rose and strode from the room swiftly, the entire Senate coming to a halt and rising in deference as her entourage rushed to catch up. There was much to think about, much to discuss, much to plan.

For she could think of only one solution to save the empire.

She had to marry Romanus Diogenes.

Dig Site

Kınalıada Island, Turkey

Present Day, Three Weeks Earlier

"Steady!"

"Sorry, Professor!"

Professor Deniz Boran shook his head as he swung from the rope, his team overhead failing to control his descent properly, the five-foot drop he had just suffered sending his heart racing as well as his body toward the floor below. He should have waited for the proper equipment to arrive from the university, but he was too eager to see what they had found. If it were what he expected, it could be the find of a lifetime, and certainly the find of his career so far.

The fabled tomb of Romanus IV Diogenes, the unlikely emperor of the Byzantine Empire who had died on this island almost one thousand years before.

A monastery once stood here, and after his betrayal, Romanus had been sent here to live out the rest of his life. What happened after his arrival wasn't exactly known. All that was known was that he never left here, and that he died either on his way, or shortly after arriving. A tragic end to a fascinating life.

What happened to his body was lost to history, but a recent discovery of a tablet, inscribed with this location apparently by Romanus' best friend, a man only known as Alexander, had Boran racing here with a team. What was odd about the tablet was the fact it was a tablet. Why would this man, who would have been accustomed to writing with pen and paper, ever inscribe something on a stone tablet?

The only explanation they had come up with, and it was pure conjecture, was that he wanted his message preserved. It was the theory Boran leaned toward, especially with the tablet's penultimate line.

Should you find my friend, treat him with the respect he deserves, and find the truth that so haunted him.

But it was the closing line that had sent a shiver down his spine.

And God have mercy on all our souls should the truth be what we feared.

A cryptic message. What did men fear a millennium ago that they were certain would terrify their descendants? Boran had no clue, though he had a feeling he would soon find out. He just hoped it didn't turn out to be something trivial that modern man would chuckle at. He wanted a mystery. He wanted something to sink his teeth into, to write papers about for years, to inspire the next generation of archaeologists.

And he wanted his colleagues in his profession green with envy.

He lived and worked in Istanbul, the former Constantinople, the greatest city in Europe for over a thousand years, yet everything had already been discovered. Yes, there were digs throughout the city as it modernized, and he and his colleagues were in high demand, but it was always the same old thing. Another building, another home, another piece of infrastructure. Yes, all important, all interesting, but all seen before.

Until last week, when the tablet was uncovered in the recently discovered home of a nobleman, buried and forgotten centuries ago—the first exciting find of his career, about to be put to shame any moment now.

His toes touched the floor then his heels. "I'm down!" he called to those overhead, the dome of what he expected was a small mausoleum arcing overhead, a large crack discovered after they had begun excavating. He had used the damaged section to make his entry sooner than they had planned—he had figured it would take weeks if not longer to excavate the entire building before they could make entry through one of its traditional entranceways.

A bit of luck, he supposed, though it was dangerous. Tons of dirt still lay overhead, putting stress on the damaged dome, and if they weren't careful, the entire thing could come down on them. It was why he had gone first, and would be the only one to step inside for now.

"What do you see?" asked Osman, one of his graduate students.

Boran untied the rope from his waist then slowly turned, the light on his helmet revealing little. He removed a flashlight from his belt and flicked it on, adding its beam to the mix.

And smiled.

In the center of the room, only feet from where he stood, sat a sarcophagus covered in centuries of dust, the top cracked by the stone that had fallen from overhead, a mound of dirt covering a portion of it and the floor surrounding it. Exactly where the tablet had indicated the final resting place of Emperor Romanus would be.

"There's a sarcophagus in the center of the room. The top is broken. It looks like the stone from the roof cave-in cracked it."

"Can you see inside?"

Boran stepped closer, playing his flashlight over the top, the crack perhaps a finger-width wide. He shone the light directly inside but could make out little. He fished out his phone then positioned the camera lens over the crack, taking several photos. He pulled the first photo up and a shiver raced down his spine. "Barely. There's a body inside though."

"Check for markings on the sarcophagus."

He chuckled, his student becoming the teacher. He stepped back from his prize to make a proper assessment. He slowly circled the find, taking photos and video, each one automatically sent into the cloud storage his students and faculty shared, oohs and ahs from overhead suggesting they were as excited as him.

Then there it was, lying beside the sarcophagus, knocked off by the collapse. A stone shield, engraved with the Byzantine double-eagle, then below it words written in Latin and Ancient Greek, both of which he could read fluently.

Here lies Romanus IV Diogenes, Emperor of the Roman Empire, betrayed and slain by his enemies, on this day of our Lord, August 4, 1072. May he rest in peace.

He took a knee, playing the light over the surface, tears filling his eyes. He had found him. He had found one of the most mysterious emperors in Roman history, the last great emperor of the Eastern Roman Empire. A man so much was known about except his final resting place.

A mystery now solved.

By him.

The ground vibrated and a fresh burst of dust erupted from overhead. He spun as a rumble echoed through the burial chamber. A stone fell nearby, shattering on the floor, and his heart leaped into his throat.

The ceiling was collapsing.

"Everyone off the roof!" he shouted as he raced for the rope. He grabbed on to it and pulled as another stone fell. He prayed the screams from overhead signaled his students and staff rushing to safety. He continued to yank on the rope, the slack still running through his hands before a shadow covered the hole above and the rope went taut.

"Hang on, Professor! I've got you!"

It was Osman.

"Get out of here, you fool! Just tie off the rope somewhere!"

"Hook yourself to the rope!"

There was no time to debate this. He reattached himself to the harness. "I'm on! Pull!"

He barely budged, his faithful student grunting overhead as the ceiling continued to collapse around him. He grabbed the rope and climbed, but his arms were too weak. Rope climbing had never been his forte in gym class, and definitely not as a slightly overweight archaeologist in his mid-forties.

He cried out as a stone slammed into his shoulder, and he dropped the few feet he had managed to climb on his own, instead now swinging slightly above the ground.

"Help me!" shouted Osman, and moments later the tugging on the rope increased as more of his pupils put their lives at risk to save him. He was in a haze of blinding pain, unable to protest. He finally recovered, enough to grab back on to the rope, and was about to warn off his students when Osman shouted from above. "Look out!"

And Boran gasped as the entire ceiling collapsed above him and he dropped back to the floor, his students, along with tons of dirt and stone, falling toward him, burying him along with Romanus, as if this place were cursed, and God desired its secrets to remain just that.

Undiscovered by man.

Great Palace of Constantinople

Constantinople, Eastern Roman Empire

AD 1067

"The traitor is right."

Empress Eudokia regarded one of her most trusted advisors, Senator Zographos, a man who had been at her late husband's side for years, predating his ascension to the throne. She valued his counsel, even when she disagreed with it. Yet today, she had a sense they were in agreement on the subject not yet mentioned. "To what do you refer?"

"Our armies are weak and our enemies are strong. Most of our soldiers are mercenaries who are only motivated by money. Give me an army of Roman citizens any day over the scum that now defend us. Romans fight for their empire, for their way of life, for their families and friends. Their motivations are things to fight to the death for. Greed merely motivates until the reward at the end is threatened. If a man is only in it for the money, and he thinks he is going to die, he retreats, he doesn't take that risk, because if he dies, he loses his money.

"When a Roman risks his life, he knows if he dies, he is doing so for his empire, for his family, for his friends. He knows if he sacrifices himself, and his fellow soldiers are able to advance because of it, he contributes to the victory that will secure his family's future. A mercenary has no such thoughts. Romanus is right. We must reconstitute our armies, especially in the east, with men willing to die to protect the empire."

Eudokia leaned to her side, curling her legs up under her as she sat in her favorite chair, a plush affair in the corner of her private office where few tread. "My husband said something similar before his death, and I agreed with him then, as I do with Romanus now. The challenge we face is rallying the citizens to the cause. As a woman, I cannot lead an army as I have no training and will command little respect. That is the job of an emperor. And my eldest has no experience, nor the temperament. At nineteen, he would command even less respect. We need a leader the people will rally behind, a leader who will have them clamoring to volunteer. We need an emperor."

Zographos' eyes narrowed. "Your Majesty, I'm not certain I understand. We do have an emperor. In fact, we have co-emperors."

"My sons are emperors in name only." She glanced over at her eldest, sitting in the opposite corner, reading something. "Wouldn't you agree, Michael?"

Michael glanced up. "Excuse me?"

"I said, you're an emperor in name only. Agreed?"

He shrugged. "Whatever you say, Mother." He returned his attention to whatever it was he was reading and she threw up her hands.

"See? There's a reason I am empress regnant, not regent. He's not fit to rule. Perhaps one day, but not today. And unfortunately, the empire needs a leader today."

Zographos leaned forward. "Then what do you propose?"

"That I be given permission to break my vow made to my husband on his deathbed, in front of too many important witnesses to simply ignore."

Zographos' eyebrows shot up. "You mean…"

Eudokia nodded, knowing full well the man was aware of what she spoke, as he had been in the room when the words were said. "I must take another husband."

Zographos shot to his feet but wisely said nothing, instead pacing for several moments, no doubt searching for the correct words that would convey his shock but not warrant his head. He finally faced her. "I agree."

It was her turn for her eyebrows to rise. "You do?"

"Yes. It's the only logical decision, however there is danger here."

"And that is?"

"The reason you made your vow."

Eudokia regarded the man, the corner of her mouth curling slightly. "And what reason was that?"

"To keep the throne in your husband's family."

She chuckled. "Yes, a man such as you would think that was the reason, though I will admit it was a consideration. At the time, it was out of love, however, yes, you are right, the future of my sons was also a factor." She sighed, staring at Michael for a moment. "Little did I know…"

18

"If you are to take a new husband, he must be chosen carefully. There must be a full vetting process that will ensure we choose a man suitable to the station, and who is willing to take on the role while understanding his true station."

"That he is a figurehead for the people, and that I remain in charge until such time as one of my sons can take over."

"Exactly. Finding such a man will be difficult."

"I have already found him."

Zographos gasped. "Your Majesty?"

"Romanus Diogenes shall be my husband and emperor."

"But…but…"

"But nothing. Bring him to me at once."

Zographos stared at her dumbfounded then bolted from the room, and she couldn't help but giggle. She loved catching the man off guard, and this was her best yet. She regarded her son. "And what do you think of my plan?"

Michael shrugged once again. "I'm sure you know what is best, Mother. We've established the fact quite clearly that I certainly don't."

She eyed him. "Do I sense discontent?"

He sighed heavily, putting down his reading. "How am I ever to become emperor if no one ever lets me make a decision?"

She smiled slightly at the poor boy. "You need experience, my son. And experience comes with time. Stick to your studies, continue your physical training, become the man I know you can be, and one day you will rule the Roman Empire, and the people will bow at your feet in adoration and respect."

"But not today."

She laughed. "No, my son, not today. But be honest with yourself. You know you're not ready, and what is needed now is a strong leader to defend the empire. When Romanus' work is done, and the empire no longer needs him, then it will be your time to rule."

"And should he not want to step aside?"

"Then I shall slit his throat myself."

Acibadem Bakirkoy Hospital

Istanbul, Turkey

Present Day

Professor Boran and his students had been lucky. Damned lucky. He had taken the worst of it, but his students had all survived with only minor scrapes and bruises. He had been buried for almost half an hour, but Osman and the others had managed to clear the dirt from his face quickly enough that he had survived. He was dug out then everyone else was properly extracted by emergency personnel from the city.

It was an embarrassing failure. He should have been more patient. He should have excavated the entire building properly, removing the weight of the dirt piled atop the dome never designed for such a load. Now, he sat in his hospital bed, nursing a cracked collarbone and a bruised ego, having just convinced his dean not to fire him, and more importantly, to allow him to continue with the dig.

"These things happen at archaeological digs. We're dealing with structures that are centuries if not millennia old. This will be a learning experience for the students."

Dean Evrin seemed doubtful. "How could this possibly be a learning experience?"

"I told them to get off the mound. If they had obeyed my orders, the roof likely wouldn't have collapsed. Instead, they insisted on attempting to pull me out. The stress on the structure of that attempt caused it to collapse. The lesson, obviously, is to obey what their professor tells them without question."

Evrin pursed his lips, shaking his head slightly as he pinched his chin. "You almost got yourself killed because you went in too soon."

"I had no choice."

Evrin's eyebrows rose. "Oh?"

"You didn't give me any funding. You said I had to take it out of the excavation fund from the original site. I'm sure you've seen the location. It will take significant funding to properly excavate that building. I saw an opportunity with the hole in the ceiling and took it. If it contained the body of Romanus Diogenes, then I knew funding would be granted."

Evrin rolled his eyes. "So, it's my fault now."

Boran smirked. "I suppose it is."

"Well, you're the only one who was injured, and you are right, your students disobeyed your orders, though some might suggest that is more a reflection on their teacher not training them properly. More importantly, the photos you took certainly suggest you found Emperor

Romanus, which is a significant discovery, and, luckily for you and the university, you now have a benefactor."

Boran's eyes narrowed. "A benefactor?"

"Your stupidity made the news, especially in archaeology circles, and an old friend of yours reached out."

"Who?"

"Professor Laura Palmer."

Boran's jaw dropped. He hadn't seen or heard from her in years. Many years. They had been colleagues, cooperating on several digs earlier in their careers, however had lost touch after the tragedy at their last shared dig where her brother had been killed. The collapse had been so bad, the area so unstable, they had never recovered the body. The last time Boran had seen Laura was at the funeral, and they hadn't spoken since.

It was the most heartbreaking experience of his career, and after the events of yesterday, apparently something he hadn't learned from.

"I haven't spoken with her in years. Not since—"

"Not since her brother died at a dig site in Jordan." Evrin wagged a finger at him. "Just as you could have died yesterday. Learn from this, my friend, because it seems you have forgotten the lesson her brother paid the ultimate price to teach you."

Boran flushed. "You're right, of course."

"Now, she and her husband have offered to fund the dig through their foundation, and all they ask in return is that when you are ready, they get a guided tour."

Boran smiled. "It would be wonderful to see her again, and I've of course heard of her husband, Professor Acton." He swung his legs out of the bed when Evrin held up a hand.

"Just where do you think you're going?"

"To the dig site. There's work to be done."

Evrin shook his head. "Get your ass back in bed. You're not going anywhere until a doctor discharges you."

"Fine. Go get one. I don't intend to be here a second longer than I have to."

Evrin sighed as he left the room. "You're going to be the death of me one of these days. You're too impetuous."

Boran didn't respond, his mind instead already making plans for what was needed at the dig site to properly excavate it safely. With Laura Palmer and her husband providing funding, they could do it properly. Yet that hadn't saved her brother all those years ago. He had been incredibly wealthy and had funded the dig, but he had still died. Boran often wondered if Laura blamed him for her brother's death. He had insisted the site was stable, yet half a mountainside had come down on her brother.

But it shouldn't have. There was no reason for it.

Yet it had.

The fact she was providing the funding must mean that either she had never blamed him, or all was forgiven. Either way, he was looking forward to seeing her again. But more importantly, he was looking forward to solving the riddle on the tablet they had discovered.

Should you find my friend, treat him with the respect he deserves, and find the truth that so haunted him. And God have mercy on all our souls should the truth be what we feared.

What could it possibly be referring to?

Great Palace of Constantinople

Constantinople, Eastern Roman Empire

AD 1067

"You realize there is only one sentence I can give you for your crimes."

Eudokia continued to assess the man that stood before her, something she had been doing from the moment he had been escorted into the room. He stood in front of her, his shoulders back, his chest thrust out, but stripped of his uniform, instead merely sporting a loincloth to maintain what little dignity he had left.

He was gorgeous.

He stirred feelings deep inside her she hadn't experienced in years, even with her husband. Yes, she had felt the same for him in the beginning, but years of marriage and children changed things, and lust became love, which was a wonderful thing.

But this was pure animal lust and it had her tingling.

Yet at this moment, she was empress, and held this man's fate in her hands.

"I do, Your Majesty."

A hint of resignation betrayed him, and it was disappointing, tarnishing the fantasy slightly. The brave warrior, who had attempted to usurp her throne, was scared. "You fear death."

For the first time since he had entered the room, he made eye contact. "I don't fear it, though I don't embrace it, Your Majesty. I am prepared to face the punishment for my perceived crimes, but I die weeping for my empire, and bitter that I failed in my duty to it."

She pursed her lips, her stomach filled with butterflies at his words. He wasn't afraid. He wasn't a coward. And he still defied her. "Perceived?"

He bowed slightly. "Forgive my choice of words, Your Majesty, but if I had succeeded and taken power, then restored the empire to its former glory, history would brand me a hero, my deeds necessary and virtuous. But I failed, therefore I will die labeled a traitor, my actions crimes. I lost, and history will judge me in accordance with that."

Her upper chest flushed for the first time in years. It was a quirk of hers that when turned on, her skin revealed the fact with red blotches. It had always embarrassed her, though her late husband had loved it.

"It shows me that I still excite you."

Guilt washed through her as her late husband's voice echoed in her head. She shouldn't feel this way about another man. She should remain loyal to her husband and his memory. Yet his first wife had died and he had remarried. Never did she have the sense that he loved her or his first wife any more or less. He loved them both, and if a man could have enough room in his heart to love two women, then so could a woman for two men. He was dead, and would always remain her first love. But there was no shame, and no guilt, in loving again.

Yet this wasn't love, though perhaps in time it might be.

"I have a proposal for you."

Romanus eyed her suspiciously. "A proposal?"

She rose from her throne and stepped toward him, the guards standing nearby shifting uncomfortably as she approached. She circled him, her eyes racing up and down his body, glistening from the midday heat. "I agree with your assessment of my empire."

His head turned ever so slightly as she came to a halt behind him, admiring his taut buttocks. "I didn't mean to offend. What has happened to our great armies long predates even your late husband."

She wanted to smack the ass revealed by the skimpy loincloth, though resisted. "You didn't offend me. A prisoner cannot offend me." She tore herself away from the view and replaced it with another, coming to a halt directly in front of him, staring him in the eyes, barely the width of a hand separating them. "I love my empire. I love my subjects. I would do anything to protect them. You do believe that, don't you?"

"Yes." It was a stuttered response. It meant he wasn't in control. It meant he just might find her attractive. She was fully aware that she was, of course. One didn't catch the eye of a potential emperor if one wasn't. And she had been blessed to maintain her figure despite giving birth multiple times. She leaned even closer, running a finger from his Adam's apple to his navel.

"Good. It's important that you understand I am willing to make any sacrifice necessary to preserve the empire for not only its subjects, but the future glory of my sons and their sons."

"I-I do, Your Majesty."

She twirled her finger around his belly button before leaning in even closer, her lips nearly touching his ear. She inhaled, his scent powerful, masculine, intoxicating. "Do you want to hear my proposal?"

His breathing had quickened with hers, and his response was a throaty whisper. "Yes, Your Majesty."

She leaned in even more, her lips touching his earlobe, her hot breath on his skin, his on her shoulder. "You are to be my husband, and rule at my side as emperor."

He gasped as she pulled away, and she suppressed a smile as she noticed his hands covering the loincloth. "I-I'm not sure I understand, Your Majesty."

She flicked her wrist at the guards. "Leave us."

She was met with confused stares.

"Now!"

The guards quickly left the room, leaving her alone with her future husband. She stepped closer to him, reaching down and taking his hands in hers, revealing his excitement. "You are to be my husband, I am to be your wife." She glanced down. "That excites you, doesn't it?"

"Y-yes. I mean, I still don't understand. I am convicted of treason. How—?"

"I am pardoning you for all your crimes. I cannot have a husband who is a convicted criminal, now can I?" She inched closer, her chest

29

brushing against his. "Will you be my husband, and rule my empire as the figurehead it needs while you rebuild our armies and crush our enemies?"

He finally lowered his gaze, staring her directly in the eyes as he grabbed her by the shoulders, his firm grip setting her heart racing and her desire afire. "I would do anything for my empire, and for its empress."

The kiss was fervent, passionate, the embrace rough, raging, and she knew from that moment on that not only did she control him, he commanded her.

A fact she could never let him know.

Acton/Palmer Residence

St. Paul, Maryland

Present Day

"You're new to this, aren't you, sir?"

Archaeology Professor James Acton blushed at his housekeeper. "Umm, is it that obvious?"

She took the vacuum from him. "Sir, it is my job to do the vacuuming. All the cleaning."

He shifted uncomfortably. Their new home was far larger than they had planned on, and it was too much for them to maintain, especially with their friend, Interpol Agent Hugh Reading, convalescing in his private suite upstairs. They now had a gardener that maintained the grounds, and a housekeeper.

And it made him uncomfortable.

He didn't like being waited on, and guilt racked him every time he saw either of their "staff," as young Tommy Granger called them, doing something he or Laura would traditionally do. "I just thought…" He paused. He wasn't certain what to say without insulting the woman.

She regarded him. "You feel bad when you see me doing my job?"

He sighed. "Yes, I suppose."

"Then you must think I'm ashamed of what I do."

His eyes bulged. "No! Oh God, that's not what I meant. I meant…" He groaned. "I don't know what I meant."

"Let me tell you, sir, I have been doing this for over twenty years. I am a hard worker, I do my job well, and when I leave work at the end of the day, I feel good about what I have done. I feel no shame in the work I do. It is honest, hard work. Please don't feel sorry for me, or feel guilty about what I do for a living. I have raised my son on my own, and send money back to help my family. I am here legally, I pay my taxes, and I obey the laws. Yes, my life is hard, but it is far better than back home in the Philippines." She sniffed, becoming misty-eyed. "Please don't make me feel bad for what I do." Her voice cracked and his wife, Archaeology Professor Laura Palmer, rushed into the room.

"Rose, dear, what did he say to you?" Laura embraced the woman, the height difference considerable.

"Nothing, ma'am. I just overreacted."

"You did no such thing," said Acton, his stomach a mess as guilt racked him. "I let my own societal prejudices lead me into thinking I should help her do a job she didn't want to do. Rose, you're absolutely correct. There is no shame in the work you do, and you should take pride in the fact you do a remarkable job. We couldn't do what you do, and thanks to you, we always come home to an impeccable home."

Laura agreed as she released the woman. "James is right. I've never seen a home so clean, and we value every little thing you do. If we've ever said or done anything to make you think otherwise, please forgive us, and if there's anything we're doing that makes you uncomfortable, just let us know."

Rose shook her head as she wiped her eyes and nose with a tissue. "I'm sorry, I'm just emotional today. My son…well, you don't need to know my problems."

Laura sat on a stool at the breakfast bar. "I want you to feel free to tell us anything. If you're going to be in our home five days a week taking care of us, then you're family. Perhaps there's some way we can help."

Rose grunted. "Not unless you can pry a teenager's bum from the couch. He plays too much video games and I'm worried about him." She batted a hand. "It's my problem to figure out. Nothing for you to worry about."

"How old is he?" asked Acton.

"Seventeen."

"College plans?"

She shrugged. "None that I know of, though he does seem to be interested in computers. I can't get him to apply, and time is running out. And, well, he needs a scholarship or bursaries or something if he's going to go. I've saved some money, but the last couple of years have hurt my savings."

Acton felt for the woman, and he could see from the concern on Laura's face she shared his feelings. "Listen. We're both professors. I work at St. Paul's University. Perhaps there is something we can do."

Rose's eyes widened. "You're professors and you can afford a house like this?"

Laura chuckled. "Well, we came into money, let's put it that way."

Acton sat beside his wife. "How about we arrange a day for me to take your son to the university? I can give him the grand tour, and if he's interested in computers, I know exactly who we should hook him up with. We have a friend named Tommy Granger who is a wizard on computers. He might be able to spark an interest in your son. I can have one of the counselors help with the application papers, and I'll make sure his tuition gets covered by one of the programs the university offers."

Rose stared at him. "You would do this?"

"Why wouldn't we? We do what we do for the children, right? You work hard for your son, and we work hard to teach the next generation."

"It takes a village." Laura patted Rose on the arm. "So, you figure out a day for that tour, James will promise to keep his mouth shut about what you do around here, and I'll go check on Hugh. Deal?"

Rose smiled. "Deal." She darted forward and hugged Laura then Acton. "I knew getting this job was a blessing. You'll be in my prayers every night."

Acton grunted. "With the trouble we keep getting in, every good word counts."

Rose eyed him, puzzled. "Trouble?"

Laura gave him a look. "He's just kidding. Our job can be dangerous sometimes."

"But you're teachers?"

"My husband fancies himself Indiana Jones."

Acton eyed her. "And my wife fancies herself Lara Croft."

Rose giggled. "You two are too funny. Movie stars!" She grabbed the vacuum cleaner that had precipitated the entire conversation. "I will get back to work now."

Acton stood. "Just let me know when you want to do that tour."

"I will, sir. Thank you. Thank you both." Rose hurried into the next room and the vacuum turned on.

"I'm going to check on Hugh," said Laura as she headed for the stairs. "Can I trust you to not put your foot in your mouth again?"

Acton shook his head. "Nope. We've established I'm an idiot. I'll come with you."

They both climbed the stairs and smiled as Rose could be heard humming a happy tune as she worked.

"I think she deserves a raise," said Acton.

"For what you put her through, I agree. Let's talk to the agency and see what can be arranged. Perhaps benefits as well. Do you think you can get her son's tuition covered?"

Acton shook his head. "I doubt it. Some of it, probably, but we'll have to take care of the rest. I don't want her to know that, though. I don't want her feeling obligated to us."

"Agreed. I'll leave that in your hands." She knocked gently on the door leading to their friend's suite, the house specifically purchased so he could vacation here, and perhaps one day retire here. "Hugh, are you decent?"

"What kind of question is that? I'm not your husband!"

Laura giggled and opened the door. Reading sat in his recliner, watching the television, some soccer match playing. "How are you feeling?"

Reading muted the game then gestured at the couch. "Still a lot of pain." He patted his chest. "The bastard really carved me up, but my strength is starting to return. That stent they put in after the heart attack just might be doing its job."

Reading had been put through the wringer a couple of weeks ago in Thailand, and was facing weeks more of recovery. He was spending it here rather than heading back to England. He didn't want his son seeing him like this, pride the determining factor in the decision.

"What did the nurse say?" asked Laura as they sat.

"She changed the bandages and said everything was looking good. No infections or complications evident, so that's good. She thinks everything will be closed up in a few days so the bandages won't be necessary anymore, and the risk of infection will be lower. I'll have some sexy scars to show for it, but it will be worth it."

Acton smiled, though his heart ached for the man who had helped save them all including so many children and innocents. His sacrifice had provided the necessary delay. "Well, you definitely will have one hell of a story to go with them. You'll drive the ladies wild."

Reading rolled his eyes. "I'm a little old for that."

Laura reached out and squeezed his hand. "Nonsense. There's someone out there for you."

"Not interested. This old man is a confirmed bachelor."

"Famous last words." Laura's phone chirped and she pulled it out. "It's Deniz Boran. Do you mind?"

Reading waved a hand. "Not at all."

She took the call and put it on speaker. "Deniz, how are you?"

"Hi, Laura. I've got news that couldn't wait until tomorrow. I'm sorry if I'm interrupting your dinner or anything. In fact, I don't even know what time it is here. It's been an exciting day."

Laura exchanged a thrilled grin with Acton. "What's happened?"

"We made entry! The excavation is complete. We were able to enter through the original doorway and install support braces and protection from anything coming down from above again."

"That's good. We don't want anyone getting hurt again. But you didn't call us just to tell us that, did you? I can hear it in your voice. You opened the sarcophagus, didn't you?"

Boran chuckled. "After all these years, you still know me too well. Yes, we were able to remove the lid. Check the cloud account. I've uploaded photos. You're going to want to see them. We'll still need to do carbon dating and further examination, but I'm quite certain we have indeed discovered the remains of Emperor Romanus IV Diogenes."

Acton indicated Reading's tablet. "May I?"

"Knock yourself out."

Acton grinned. "Look at you, becoming all American."

Reading was about to retort when he thought better of it. "You're lucky I'm stuck in this chair."

Acton logged into the cloud account then brought up the photos, holding the tablet so all could see. He flicked through the various shots of the dig, including the safety infrastructure, then the all-important opened sarcophagus. "Incredible. You're doing an amazing job, Deniz."

"Thank you, Jim. That means a lot coming from you."

Acton flipped again then paused at a closeup of a stone tablet that appeared as if it had been buried with the man, gripped by both hands. Writing was etched on it. "What can you tell us about this tablet?"

"Not much yet. It's in Hebrew. We've sent some photos out for translation."

"Give me a sec." Acton pulled out his phone and launched Tommy Granger's app that did instant translations. He had paid the young man to add ancient languages, and it had proven convenient at times, mostly for research. Today, it might pay for itself on a live dig. He snapped a photo of the tablet and the app went to work, producing a text a few moments later. "Holy shit!"

"What?" asked everyone at once.

Acton reread the translation, shaking his head. "This has to be a fake. Are you sure this was buried with him? I mean, someone didn't add it after the fact?"

"Why? What does it say?" asked Boran.

Acton handed the translation to Laura and her hand darted to her mouth as her eyes bulged. "It has to be fake," she whispered, handing the phone to Reading, who eyed it skeptically.

"Bollocks."

Acton took the phone and sent the translation to Boran. "Check your email. I just sent you the translation."

38

"How did you get…" The man's voice trailed off as he read the email. "Oh my God! Is this…could this…I mean…" There was a long pause. "I don't know what to say. I'm Muslim, so we believe this to be true, regardless. What do you Christians think?"

"This Christian thinks it's bollocks," muttered Reading.

Acton wasn't a religious man, though did believe in the broad strokes of Christianity, and if what this tablet claimed was true, it changed everything. "I think we have to determine the truth. Immediately."

"I…I think you're right," murmured Boran. "Umm, do you think we could be in danger?"

Laura nodded, no doubt thinking of the Unus Veritas Chest containing a manifest of all that had been hidden away by the Catholic Church over a millennium, hidden in the Vault of Secrets beneath the Vatican. "If word gets out that you have found something that challenges the core belief of Christianity, then yes."

"What should we do?"

"Arrange security immediately. Let me know what funding you need, but get it arranged now, not tomorrow. And secure that tablet immediately. And tell your team not to share any photos of it. We can't risk it going public."

"I'm afraid it's too late for that."

Acton tensed. "What do you mean?"

"Dozens if not hundreds of photos are already up on social media. This discovery is already big news. It just never occurred to us that the tablet would prove so…controversial."

Laura stared at Acton. "Then it might already be too late."

Acton agreed. "I'm going there. I've got more experience in these types of things."

"I'll go too."

Acton shook his head. "No, somebody has to stay with Hugh."

"Like hell they do," protested their friend.

Laura gave him a look. "James will go tonight, and I'll arrange full-time care for you then I'll join him."

Reading growled. "I hate feeling like an invalid."

Acton sent a text message to their head of security, Cameron Leather, a former lieutenant colonel in the British Special Air Service. "I'm contacting Cam. I'll see if he can have a team meet us in Istanbul."

Reading stared at him. "What? This is all happening in Istanbul? You do realize that their government isn't exactly that friendly anymore."

"We've gone into far worse places."

Reading sighed heavily. "Curse that Thai bastard for doing this to me!"

"Hey, that Thai bastard probably saved your life. If you hadn't had that heart attack with all the right equipment on hand, you'd be dead."

"Bollocks!"

Acton leaned closer to Laura's phone. "I'm coming there as soon as I can. I'll send you the details. Secure that tablet, arrange your own security, and try to scrub anything you can off the Internet."

"I'm on it," replied Boran. "Let's just hope it's not too late."

Great Palace of Constantinople

Constantinople, Eastern Roman Empire

AD 1068

Eudokia cried out in ecstasy as Romanus roared his climax, the simultaneous release the perfect ending to a momentous day. Earlier, they had been married, then to complete the ceremony, her new husband was crowned emperor. After the celebrations attended by the who's who of Roman society and dignitaries from afar, had come the consummation of her greatest negotiation since becoming empress.

And she had no regrets.

Romanus was voracious. It might have been because he was drunk with the power he now had, the near omnipotence fueling his domination over her body, or he might have always been this way. Whatever the reason, she didn't care. She was satisfied in every way. As a woman sexually, as a mother who had secured her sons' futures, and a leader who had saved her empire.

Yet tonight was merely formality. The real work began tomorrow. Rebuilding their army.

Romanus rolled off her then propped his head up on a pillow, staring at her with a smile. "You were wonderful."

She returned the smile. "So were you."

"I have a question for you."

"Of course."

"Shall we make an effort to have children of our own?"

She regarded him for a moment. Avoiding children would mean depriving herself of what had just occurred, something she absolutely wanted to enjoy again. Repeatedly. And any children they might have would be far too young to be a challenge for her own sons for at least two decades. She could see no reason not to bear this man's children. "I am willing if you are."

He leaned in and kissed her, pulling her body tight against his. "Oh, I'm willing." He pulled away slightly. "But should any be sons, they must be named co-emperor upon birth. Agreed?"

"As mine already are, and remain."

"Of course, and when they are ready, I will enjoy their counsel. Until then—"

"You shall obey mine."

He pushed her onto her back and mounted her. She gasped, her eyes bulging as he grabbed her by the shoulders. "Am I to be your consort, or you mine?"

She moaned. "In the bed, I am yours, but outside of it, you are mine."

He continued his dominion, much to her delight, all the while staring into her eyes. "Agreed. Tomorrow, with your permission, I will begin reconstituting our armies, concentrating on the east. It will take many months, but as soon as we are ready, I will lead them myself into battle, leaving the empire to you to run while I secure its borders. Does this please you?"

She smirked. "Your plan, or what you're doing now."

He grinned. "Both."

She closed her eyes and sighed. "Your empress is pleased."

Corpo della Gendarmeria Office

Palazzo del Governatorato, Vatican City

Present Day

Inspector General Mario Giasson yawned then stretched, groaning as he did so. It was late, past his usual quitting time, but his mother-in-law was visiting, and he had made up an excuse to stay away. The woman hated him, and he wasn't about to spend any more time with her than he had to. Thankfully, she was leaving tomorrow morning, and peace would once again be restored in the Giasson household.

He glanced at his watch. Twelve more hours, over half of that asleep. He could manage that without tearing his hair out. He wiped his hand over his shaved scalp, wondering if subconsciously that was why he had done away with it.

Alfredo Ianuzzi tapped on his door and Giasson waved him in. "What is it?"

Ianuzzi, one of his senior team members, held up a large, thin envelope. "This was just delivered by messenger."

"What is it?"

Ianuzzi stepped over and handed it to him. "It's marked 'personal and confidential.' I figured you wouldn't want anyone seeing it but you."

Giasson examined the envelope. He couldn't recall the last time he had seen anything labeled as such addressed to him, though the Vatican certainly received its fair share, usually containing threats from crackpots hoping to directly reach the Pope or one of the senior officials. Few knew, however, that this office even existed.

"It's been scanned, in case you're wondering. Nothing detected."

Giasson retrieved his letter opener then slid it through one end, slicing the envelope open. He held it away from him and drew a deep breath, holding it as he gently gave the envelope a shake. A single piece of paper slid out slightly, with no powder or other substance accompanying it. He relaxed slightly and tugged the rest of the page out.

And his eyebrows shot up.

"This can't be good."

Ianuzzi leaned forward. "What is it?"

Giasson held up the page for his subordinate to see. It contained the upside-down cross of St. Peter with two crossed keys, a photo underneath of what appeared to be an ancient stone tablet, then a warning.

Do not interfere.

Ianuzzi's eyes narrowed. "Do not interfere? Interfere in what?"

Giasson shook his head. "I don't know, but this"—he tapped the cross—"means trouble. Close the door." Ianuzzi complied as Giasson pulled out his cellphone. "This is the symbol of the Keepers of the One Truth."

Ianuzzi's jaw dropped. "Holy shit!" He slapped a hand over his mouth. "I'm sorry, sir, but I thought we were done with them?"

"We'll never be done with them, and if they're involved in something, we have to be very careful. They're the kind of trouble that doesn't worry about killing to get their way."

"But what is this all about?"

Giasson took a photo of the page then texted it to the only people he could trust to give him an answer without putting anyone in the Vatican at risk. "I don't know, but I'm about to find out."

Acton/Palmer Residence

St. Paul, Maryland

"Cameron says he can have a team in Istanbul by the time James arrives."

Reading's head bobbed at Laura's update. "That's good. I'll feel a lot better if he's there with him. I don't trust the situation."

Laura regarded her friend. "What do you mean?"

"Let's face it. Turkey has been lost to the fundamentalists. If word gets out that there's an artifact that proves Christianity is bullshit, the nutbars will be lining up to get their hands on it."

Laura tensed. Reading was right. It was an unfortunate truth that there were people on both sides that were determined to undermine the beliefs of the opposing side, and what was written on the tablet discovered in Romanus' tomb was unfathomably shocking. It didn't matter whether it was fake. People would kill to either preserve it so they could prove it true, or destroy it to hide its secrets.

Either way, her husband was once again heading toward the danger. If anything happened, it would be interpreted as his own fault, so help might not be available.

And she was determined to join him as soon as possible.

Fulltime nursing had been arranged for tomorrow morning, and she would be twelve hours behind her husband. An eternity should something go wrong.

"What's on your mind?" asked Reading, his voice gentle.

She sighed. "Sometimes I wonder if it's our responsibility to get involved in these things. I mean, there's no real need for us to go to Istanbul. We gave Deniz the necessary advice. With security arranged and the tablet safely stored, what more is there that needs to be done? I mean, do we really need to be there for that?"

Reading smiled at her. "I'm happy to see you've finally come over to my way of thinking."

"Perhaps."

"Perhaps?"

She sighed. "I realize it's not our responsibility, but perhaps it's our duty."

"Duty? How the devil do you figure that?"

"What if it's true?"

Reading paused, staring at her. "You don't believe it is, do you?"

"I don't know." She shivered. "But what if it is? It changes everything."

"Does it?"

Her eyes shot wide. "Doesn't it? I mean, if what it says is actually true, then everything Christians have believed in for two millennia is wrong. The entire thing has been a hoax. Everything is…"

"Bullshit?"

She shrugged. "For lack of a better word, yes."

"So, what if it is?"

"Huh?"

Reading leaned slightly closer, wincing. "So, what if it is? I mean, we're in the twenty-first century now. I think society is mature enough to survive the collapse of a religion."

She shook her head. "I don't have the faith in society you do. And remember, we're from England. In Europe, the church is something that has been gradually pushed into the background. Here, they still have 'In God We Trust' on their currency, and continue to argue over whether the Ten Commandments can be displayed on government property. And let's not forget the Third World where Christianity reigns supreme. What will people who truly, deeply believe in what they've been taught their entire lives, do when they hear this? Will they just accept it and move on, or will they challenge it? And if they challenge it, will they attempt to silence anyone who accepts the truth? And what is the truth? Could we ever prove what the tablet says? What if the tablet itself is a hoax? Will people try to destroy the knowledge so it doesn't risk undermining their beliefs?"

Reading sighed, easing back in his chair, wincing once again. "You may be right, which is why it is all the more important to handle this delicately, perhaps by people who are comfortably distant from the true believers."

Laura eyed him. "You mean like James and I."

"I hate to say it, but yes. This has the possibility of turning into a religious war. If one side gets their hands on it and claims Christianity is bunk, Christians the world over could go apeshit, as Jim might say, and begin killing Muslims. And if the Christians find out first, they could go after whoever has it, and kill them so that the word never gets out. This has to be handled very carefully, or a lot of people could die."

Laura's shoulders slumped. "I never thought I'd see the day where you'd be the one urging us to head toward the danger."

"Sometimes it *is* our duty to put our lives at risk for the greater good. It's why I became a police officer, and it's why, I believe, you two have been training so intensely for years so that you're prepared for situations like this. What other archaeologists do you know that could handle themselves if things got violent?"

Laura groaned. "Indiana Jones and Lara Croft." She glanced down at the girls. "I don't think I can fill her shoes."

"Shoes?"

Laura gasped. "Hugh! You're terrible!"

Reading laughed then pressed against his wounds. "I'm sorry. I couldn't resist."

"Uh-huh." Laura's phone demanded attention and she picked it up from the table, her eyes narrowing.

"What is it?"

"A message from Mario Giasson." She brought it up and her jaw dropped. "Oh no!"

Reading leaned over, despite the pain. "What is it?"

She held up the phone so he could see the image showing the symbol for the Keepers of the One Truth, an organization they had run into on several occasions, and never with a good outcome. But it was the image of the tablet and the warning that had her more concerned.

"What does it say?" asked Reading, unfamiliar with Italian.

"Do not interfere."

Reading closed his eyes for a moment. "Sometimes I hate it when I'm right."

"What do we do?"

"Call Jim right away and tell him to get his ass back here."

"But what about what we were just talking about?"

Reading shook his head. "If those guys are involved, it's already too late. Better to let them take the tablet and hide it away, than to interfere."

She dialed James' satphone, but it went to voicemail. "James, call me as soon as you get this. It's urgent." She hung up. "Straight to voicemail."

Reading cursed. "Let's reach out to Mario and to your friend. If we can't reach him in the air, then we'll have to intercept him on the ground."

Laura's hands shook and she took a calming breath before dialing Giasson's number.

The man answered immediately. "Laura, thank you for getting back to me. I need to know—"

"Listen, Mario, James could be in trouble. I need to know what you know."

"And I need to know what you know. Tell me about this tablet."

"I'm sending you the translation now." She brought up the message and sent the translation through. "Do you have it?"

"Give me a moment." She could hear Giasson typing on his keyboard then a curse erupted. "Oh my God! They'll kill everyone!"

Great Palace of Constantinople

Constantinople, Eastern Roman Empire

AD 1068

Eudokia caressed her round stomach, smiling to herself as she wondered whether she carried a son who would one day be emperor, or a daughter who might one day rule as she now did. She would be pleased with either, however a son would be preferable to ensure the family's hold over the empire.

For while her new husband had been out on campaigns in the east, forces plotted against him in Constantinople and the central territories where the noble families resided. Her late husband's family, the Doukai, were furious she had remarried, weakening the family's claim to the throne. Constantine X had been the first in their line to rule, and they had hoped it was just the beginning of a dynasty that could rule for centuries through his sons and their sons yet to be born.

Yet with Romanus now officially emperor, despite her sons being co-emperors, the Doukai were no longer confident in their hold on the throne, especially now that she was with child. Meeting after meeting had been held over the past months while her new husband fought for the empire, and she struggled to convince her in-laws their future was secure merely due to the fact the eldest son was barely twenty, and Romanus' yet to be born.

Unfortunately, her assurances fell on deaf ears, and she feared what would come should her new husband falter. For now, after an initial stumble caused by attacking too soon, he had successfully reclaimed lost territory and pushed their enemies to the east back. The empire's citizens loved him and her as well, and as long as he remained victorious, and the spoils of war continued to arrive in caravans that paraded through the cities, he was safe. Success was their greatest protection from those who would do them harm.

Her son, Michael, entered the room, eying her stomach before sitting, saying nothing.

"Is something on your mind, my son?"

He frowned before indicating her stomach. "You realize as soon as he is born, I become nothing."

She rubbed her belly. "And what if it is a girl?"

He grunted. "Obviously, you aren't aware of my luck. It will be a boy and he will be emperor."

"You are already emperor, and will be twenty years his senior. You have nothing to fear."

"I am emperor in name only, and you know that. Before you married, you were emperor. You didn't trust me to rule."

She gave him a look. "You weren't ready to rule. You still aren't ready to rule, and you know it. It is why you spend so many hours with the tutors, so you will eventually take over from me when I feel you are ready."

He laughed. "You forget you have a husband now. As long as he lives, I will never be emperor. By marrying him, you have sealed my fate, and the fate of the Doukai family's claim to the throne."

She regarded him for a moment. "Who have you been speaking with?"

He shifted in his chair. "What do you mean?"

"Someone is putting these thoughts in your head. You were never concerned with such things before."

"I'm twenty now. It's time I thought of my future."

She pursed her lips. Something was wrong. Her son had shown little interest in the throne, content to let her rule after his father's death, and had expressed his understanding of how important his continuing education was.

Something twigged. Zographos had reported earlier in the week that Caesar John Doukas had been seen in the palace, yet he hadn't paid her a visit as was customary. The awarded title of Caesar had gone to the man's head. Unlike the days of old when a Caesar meant Emperor, it was no longer so in Roman Constantinople. It was awarded by the emperor to sons or relatives with little hope of inheriting the throne, or as a reward for loyalty.

It was bad form for the man to not pay his respects.

"Caesar John visited you, didn't he?"

55

Another shift and a turn of the head away from her.

"Tell me the truth."

Still no response.

"Now!" she snapped.

Michael flinched. "Yes."

"When?"

"Two days ago."

"Where?"

"In my chambers."

"And what was said?"

Another hesitation before he turned to face her, his eyes pools of tears. "Nothing of importance, I swear! He merely asked me how I felt to no longer be the true emperor, and how I felt that Father's family had been forced out of the empire's future with your betrayal."

Her entire body shook with rage. It was one thing to make such claims to her, but to her son? It was inexcusable. Yet was it? He was a man, though barely, and was to rule one day. Difficult conversations couldn't be avoided when leader, and he needed to get used to that fact. But still, for John to do such a thing was beyond the pale. He was family, and to talk in such a way to a boy about his mother was unforgivable.

But a question had to be asked. She drew a slow breath, steadying her rage. "Do you believe I betrayed your father?"

Michael turned away once again. "You made a promise to him, then you broke that promise."

"I did it for you. I did it so that there would be an empire left for you to rule when you are ready."

"Nonsense."

The response took her aback and she recoiled from the venomous tone. "Nonsense?"

"I've seen you two when you think you're alone. You love him. More than I ever saw you love Father."

Now the truth of the matter was emerging. This had nothing to do with her son's future on the throne, and everything to do with a perceived betrayal of his father—and not the betrayal of a promise made on the man's deathbed. "Michael, I loved your father. Deeply."

"Don't lie! He's been dead barely a year, yet you carry another man's child!"

She pursed her lips. "Perhaps one day, when you love someone and lose them, you'll understand that the heart has the capacity to love more than one person. But you've never loved, so you can't understand how it works. I loved your father, and I still love him. There's not a day that goes by where I don't think of him, and wish he were here. But he's not, and there's nothing you or I can do about that. The promise I made to your father not to marry again had to do with love, but also with preserving the throne for you and your brother. It was a promise I was happy to make because I love you both, and at the time, your father and I both believed it was the right decision.

"What you may not realize, is that it was his idea, not mine. He was always thinking of his empire, and your future, as was I, and as *am* I. Our enemies are growing stronger, and we are being challenged on all sides with an army that can't defend us, nor in some cases can be trusted to as they are paid mercenaries. People like your Uncle John began plotting behind our backs almost immediately, and the discord among the noble families has been growing. My advisors and I agreed that I would need to remarry to install a military emperor on the throne to save the empire. You have to understand, that the decision was political, not emotional."

"Yet you carry his child and cavort with him like some schoolgirl."

She sighed, shaking her head. "Yes, in time I have come to love Romanus. I don't deny that. Would you rather your mother be miserable and alone for the rest of her life? Or would you rather see her happy, remembering that she still loves your father as much as she ever did, but accepts the fact he is gone, long before his time?"

Michael's shoulders shook as he buried his head in his hands. "I miss Father so much!"

She hurried to his side and wrapped her arms around him, holding him tight. "And I miss him too. You must believe me."

"I-I don't know what to believe anymore. Uncle John said some horrible things, and I fear he means to do you and Romanus harm."

She bristled, pushing back slightly and taking her son by the chin, directing his eyes toward hers. "Tell me exactly what he said. Leave no detail out."

Istanbul Ataturk Airport

Istanbul, Turkey

Present Day

Acton stepped onto the tarmac, an experience he was still getting used to. Flying around the world on private jets thanks to his wife's membership in a lease-share network was a delight, but there was still something to be said about the airconditioned jetway that protected one from the elements.

Like the oppressive heat he now suffered, something his friend Reading would be already cursing.

The thought of his friend had him concerned. Reading was recovering from his ordeal in Thailand, but it would be a long haul. The physical wounds would heal, though the scars would be a constant reminder of what had been done to him. His heart would recover now that the stent had been inserted and his physical therapy regimen had begun. It was the psychological scars that Acton was concerned about. On several occasions they had heard him crying out in the night, as if waking from nightmares they could only imagine. Laura had tried to talk to their friend about it, but he had refused, and had refused the offer of a therapist.

He was too damned proud.

Reading was old school, too old school for his own good sometimes. They had discussed it and decided the best thing to do was to continue with the convalescence, have him physically recover, then make another attempt at the psychological once more time had passed. It was all they could do.

A young woman from the charter terminal hailed him with a smile. "Professor Acton! Welcome to Istanbul. If you would follow me, I'll get you cleared through customs. I believe your driver is already here."

Acton followed her. "My driver?"

"Yes, someone from a university I believe. I'm sorry, I can't remember which one. You weren't expecting them?"

"Frankly, it hadn't been discussed. I was just going to rent a vehicle."

"Well, it looks like they're giving you the royal treatment. You won't need to."

Acton chuckled. "I prefer to drive myself, but I'm not familiar with the streets here, so maybe it's for the best."

She laughed as she held open the door for him. "A man with a private jet that prefers to drive himself. Wonders never cease."

Acton quickly cleared customs, one of the best perks of private jet travel, then was directed to a man in a chauffeur's uniform.

"Professor Acton?"

"Yes."

"I'm Kenan. I've been contracted by the university to take you anywhere you need to go during your stay here."

"Terrific. I guess the first stop should be my hotel, then once I'm freshened up, we'll probably be going to the dig site. Do you know where that is?"

"Yes, sir. I've been given all the key destinations by the university. You're in good hands, sir."

Acton smiled. "Happy to hear it." He followed the man outside, a porter bringing his luggage, and immediately doubted the claim of good hands when he spotted the vehicle that was to transport him around the city. An SUV built by a notorious British carmaker. He kept his mouth shut and climbed in the back as the luggage was loaded. He put on his seatbelt and examined his surroundings. He had to admit they were plush, certainly far nicer than his beater, but you could put lipstick on a pig of an electrical system, and it was still a pig of an electrical system.

Kenan climbed in the driver's seat then pulled them away from the curb, merging into the airport traffic. "I'll give you some privacy, sir."

A panel rose, separating them, the vehicle obviously customized for its purpose, and Acton sank his head back into the sumptuous leather, closing his eyes. A hissing sound had him sitting up and opening his eyes, searching for the source. He spotted smoke coming from the floor and immediately his thoughts turned to the car having caught on fire, just as he would expect from a piece of shit like this.

He slammed his fist on the divider. "There's smoke coming in back here!"

But there was no response.

61

He tried to open the window but it wouldn't work, then he tried the door handle to no avail. He held his breath as long as he could as he continued to hammer on the divider then attempted to break the window with his elbow. His lungs screamed in agony as they burned, demanding oxygen, and finally he gave up, gasping in lungsful of air, the mist that now surrounded him inhaled rapidly with none of the effects he would expect from smoke.

This was no electrical fire.

And he was being ignored on purpose.

He became drowsy within seconds before finally passing out, wondering just who Kenan was, and who he worked for.

He was definitely not from the university.

Acton/Palmer Residence

St. Paul, Maryland

Laura paced back and forth in front of Reading, a thumbnail clamped firmly in her teeth. The conversation with Giasson had been terrifying. If the Keepers of the One Truth were aware of the tablet, then James was in trouble. They had essentially ordered the Vatican to not interfere with their warning to the Inspector General, and from what Giasson had said, they wouldn't get involved.

They couldn't. The Vatican, while officially a country, didn't interfere in things such as this, though Giasson had indicated he would contact his counterpart in Ankara. He didn't hold out much hope, however, since things in Turkey were turning more fundamentalist by the day since the election of Erdogan. Any hope that country ever had of joining the European Union was dead, and she was certain politicians the continent over were thankful they had never agreed to let them join, since this was exactly what they had feared.

But none of that helped her now. If the Turkish authorities wouldn't cooperate, then they were on their own. She could only hope they still believed in law and order, and that they would do the right thing, despite the warning coming from their religious rivals.

She growled. Nine times out of ten the problems of this world seemed tied to religion, though perhaps that wasn't fair. China and North Korea had no official religion, and Russians were just led by a lunatic.

And again, her thoughts were of no help.

"Sit down. You're going to wear a hole in the rug."

She paused, stared at Reading for a moment, then sat. "I feel so helpless."

"He just landed. He'll get your messages and take precautions. He's a smart man."

"He's a smart man who despite that, does stupid things."

"Pot, meet kettle."

She glared at him then laughed. "You're right. I'm no better." She checked her phone again, and it still indicated the messages hadn't been received yet. It didn't make sense. As soon as he had landed his phone should have connected to the local cellular network and his messages should have come through.

Something was wrong.

"Could they already know he was coming?"

Reading shrugged. "We have no idea how well connected they are. They had a deep-cover operative in the Vatican once before, and I have no doubt they still do. Someone from inside Mario's office could be feeding them everything. They might not have known when Jim got in the air, but they probably knew by the time he landed."

"And if they did know, what do you think they would do?"

Reading sighed. "There's no reason to harm him, at least not initially. They would probably warn him off somehow. Threaten him."

"But shouldn't we have still heard from him? I can't see them abducting him at the airport."

"Remember Rome? You two were abducted right off the tarmac."

She shivered at the memory. It wasn't the Keepers that had kidnapped them, but it was the same event that introduced them. "I'm worried. Really worried."

"Check the flight."

She did again, and it confirmed what she already knew. It had landed on schedule, in fact, a few minutes before. Plenty of time had already passed for him to clear customs and to get a rental, though perhaps there had been trouble there. "Maybe they were out of cars, so he's waiting."

Reading nodded. "Definitely possible, though it doesn't explain why his messages haven't been received."

"Perhaps he forgot to charge his phone and it's dead."

"That's a definite possibility. Right now, we could be worrying about nothing."

A thought occurred to Laura that had her dialing Mary, their travel agent.

"Hello, Laura, what can I do for you?"

"Hi Mary, I can't reach James. There's a situation developing and I need to reach him. The computer says he landed almost twenty minutes ago, but—"

"I'm on it. I'll call you back in a few minutes."

"Thank you." She ended the call then turned to Reading. "If anyone can find out, it's her."

Reading grunted. "I still want to know who she is. That woman is far too well connected to just be a travel agent."

"Like I said, she worked for my brother then offered her services to me. Other than that, I've never even met her. She's just a voice on the other end of the phone."

"Mysteriouser and mysteriouser."

"You detectives and your suspicious minds."

"You're not suspicious?"

She shrugged. "Why look a gift horse in the mouth? She does amazing things for us, so why pry? If she wanted us to know, she'd tell us. Right now, I'm just happy she's on our side."

Her phone rang and she held it up so he could see the call display.

It was Mary.

Laura answered and put it on speaker so Reading could hear. "Hi, Mary, did you find out anything?"

"I did, and you're not going to like it."

A lump formed in Laura's throat as her stomach flipped. "What?" she asked, her voice barely a murmur.

"Your husband landed, cleared customs, then was taken by a chauffeur from the university."

66

Laura's eyes narrowed. "A chauffeur? He was supposed to arrange a rental. There was no vehicle arranged by the university."

"You're right, there wasn't. I called Professor Boran and he confirmed no driver had been sent. He said there was no budget for such things."

"Then who picked up James?"

"I don't know, but whoever it was had help."

Reading leaned closer. "This is Hugh Reading. What do you mean?"

"His phone was never registered to the cellular network in Istanbul. That means there was some sort of jammer blocking the signal. His driver couldn't have done that, since he'd be inside the terminal, and anything strong enough to reach the tarmac would have taken out too many phones not to be noticed. It had to be somebody in close proximity to Mr. Acton."

Laura thought back on their previous experiences at private terminals. "Like the greeter." She gasped. "Or the porter! He would have been out there waiting to take the luggage, then followed them into the terminal then to the car."

"Either is a definite possibility. Either way, it means this was well-organized by people who knew where and when your husband would be there, with enough time to plan this."

Laura blanched. "The Keepers of the One Truth."

"Who?"

"Nothing. Umm, keep us posted if you hear anything else. And see if you can move up that flight for me to Istanbul."

"Understood. There's one other thing you should know about."

"What's that?"

"Your security team's plane was delayed leaving Cairo. They just landed five minutes ago."

Reading frowned. "That seems far too coincidental."

"With what you've told me, yes, it does."

Laura picked up the phone. "Thanks for your help, Mary. Get back to me when the flight is arranged."

"Will do. And one more thing?"

"Yes?"

"Next time you need to reach your husband urgently on a plane, call me. I could have simply contacted the pilot."

Laura sighed. "You're right. I guess I'm still thinking in terms of what is possible on a commercial flight. Next time, I call. Thanks." She ended the call and Reading laid into her immediately.

"You're still going to Istanbul? Are you daft?"

"I have to find James."

"It's too dangerous."

She shook her head. "No, Cameron will be there with his team. I'll be perfectly safe."

"Just like Jim was supposed to be."

"He wasn't supposed to meet them until the hotel. Nobody thought anything could go wrong until the dig site. This was supposed to be possible fundamentalists attacking the site, not a conspiracy by a well-organized cult."

Reading sighed, slamming his head against the back of his chair. "I wish I could go with you." He moved to get up. "In fact—"

"You'll do no such thing! Sit your ass back in that chair and accept your situation. As much as it pains me to say it, you and I both know that you'll just be a liability."

Reading sat back down and turned his face away. Her heart ached and she rose, taking a knee beside him them squeezing his hand. "I'm useless."

Her eyes filled with tears at the proud man's admission. "You're not useless. You saved us all, and now you're paying a temporary price. You'll be back to your old self in no time. Unfortunately, with the frequency James and I get in trouble, it just means you'll have to sit out a few of our mishaps."

He faced her, his eyes red. "You two should just stay put for a couple of months. Enjoy your new home and let the world sort out its own problems."

She shrugged. "Where would be the fun in that?" She kissed his hand then rose, returning to her seat. "I do have an idea, however."

"What's that?"

"Your body may not be able to help, but your mind can."

His eyes narrowed. "Help out an old man."

"If we're battling the Keepers, and they're that well-connected in Istanbul, then we're going to need help."

"Dylan and his friends?"

"Oh, I'm definitely contacting them, but sometimes help a little closer to home is preferable."

"What do you mean?"

"I'm thinking we get Tommy and Mai over here and we set up a little operations center of our own."

Reading smiled broadly. "Brilliant."

Unknown Location

"Is he awake?"

"Yes. He's just faking being asleep."

Acton suppressed the frown at his captors' discovery. He had been listening for several minutes to a whispered conversation between two men. He could barely hear them and had given up when he realized it was all in Italian, though the last two sentences were spoken in English, likely for his benefit. The subterfuge, however, had given him the opportunity to clear the fog that clouded his mind, and assess his situation. He could feel the bindings holding his feet and hands to the chair he sat in, and other than a slight feeling of nausea, probably from whatever gas they had used on him, he felt fine.

The question was, who were they? The Italian had thrown him off, but as he thought about it, he could come to only one conclusion, and it was a terrifying one. It had to be the Keepers of the One Truth. They were a cult, for lack of a better word, that claimed to have been founded by St. Peter himself, to protect the Church from anything that might bring it harm.

And he had killed several of its members.

He opened his eyes then blinked several times to allow them to focus. Two men stood in front of him, neither of whom he recognized. He took a gamble. "What do the Keepers of the One Truth want with me today?"

The reaction was what he had hoped for. Surprise. It meant they were who he suspected, and they hadn't expected him to know. It meant that he could play this to his advantage, and perhaps convince him that others knew as well. It might just get him out of this alive.

"A good guess, Professor Acton," said the man whose voice he recognized as the one in charge, at least of the two in this room. "I suspect your deductive reasoning skills brought you to that conclusion, considering we didn't become involved until you were already in the air."

"That may be so, however, before I left, your organization was one of the ones we were concerned about getting involved. Trust me when I say that if anything happens to me, my friends will know who to come after."

The man chuckled. "I've heard about you, Professor, and the stories certainly weren't exaggerated. It's a wonder you can walk with balls so big."

Acton grinned. "It's a struggle, but I manage."

The man batted a hand. "You're not here so we can hurt you. You're here because we need your help."

Acton hid his surprise. "Oh?"

"You are here because of the tablet."

"I think it's safe to admit that."

"And you of course know what it says, since you provided the translation."

"Yes."

"And you must be aware that this blasphemy cannot be allowed to stand."

Acton regarded the man, choosing his words carefully. "It's only blasphemous if it's not the truth."

The other man gasped and opened his mouth to say something when the leader cut him off with a raised hand. "Do you believe it's the truth?"

"There's no way to know for certain without investigating."

"And that's exactly what we want you to do."

"Excuse me?"

"I assume you intend to visit the location indicated on the tablet?"

"I would like to, however it appears to be in Syria. Not an easy country to get into at the moment."

"We'll get you in."

Acton regarded the man. "You'll get me in, but that doesn't mean it's safe to be there."

"That's not our concern. We'll get you in, you find the location indicated, then we'll prove this tablet is a fake, and all will return to normal."

"And if it isn't?"

"It is!" cried the other. "If it isn't, it means it is all a lie, and I refuse to believe that!"

The leader calmed the man. "We know it to be fake, but we must have proof, otherwise it could trigger a holy war. Think about it, a tablet that makes such an outlandish claim is discovered by a Muslim on Muslim territory? Christians the world over will be outraged, and when their faith is challenged by those who have none, or by those who want to stir up trouble like the fundamentalists, there will be violence on the streets. Thousands if not millions could die in the end. Do you really want that to happen?"

Acton frowned. The man was right, and it was already something they had considered. This was a dangerous situation, exactly why he had wanted Leather here.

Next time he meets you at the airport, no matter how safe you think the country is.

"No, I don't think any of us want that."

"Good. Then you'll cooperate?"

"If I say yes, then what happens?"

"We let you go."

"Then what stops me from just getting back on an airplane and washing my hands of this entire situation."

"Because we'll kill your wife in a most horrendous way."

Acton bristled. If anyone was capable, and had proven a willingness to kill, it was the Keepers. He couldn't risk it, and besides, all they were asking him to do was what he would have done regardless. He sighed. "Very well, we have a deal."

Hierapolis

AD 1068

The Emir of Aleppo, Rashid al-Dawla Mahmud, pressed against the wall then peered out the window at the sight below. It was both terrifying and heartbreaking. The Romans were inside the mighty walls of Hierapolis and were in the process of sacking the city. He had failed to defend her, yet he would have his revenge, and was convinced his enemy's victory would be short-lived.

He had an army of almost 20,000 amassing to the south.

These infidels and their Christian nonsense would ultimately lose, but that wasn't enough. He wanted to destroy their faith, and he had the means.

And it was why he had let them win.

The grand Roman Army might very well have won in the end, however he had ordered the weakening of the main gate, allowing the Romans to batter their way through far quicker than they might have otherwise. It was all part of a calculated plan he had hatched once he received word the Romans were again on the move.

A brilliant plan, if he did say so himself.

"Sir, we must leave now if we are to make it to the tunnel in time."

Mahmud glanced over his shoulder at his most trusted advisor, Jalal. The man stood in the doorway as calm as he had ever seen him, as if the fact the Romans were piling dirt around the walls to raise ramps high enough to gain entry was of no consequence. He was remarkable, and on many occasions his level head had kept Mahmud from rash decisions.

And if Jalal said it was time, then it was.

"Where is the tablet?"

Jalal gestured toward the inner office. "On your desk, as instructed."

Mahmud headed for the door. "Good. It is essential they find this little piece of history we have for them." He entered his office and stood behind his desk, running his hand over the tablet, the Hebrew writing etched into its surface incomprehensible to him. Yet he knew the words, and the effect they would have on these Christians who would dare shed the blood of Allah's soldiers.

But in the heat of war, soldiers could do stupid things, and a Hebrew tablet could be destroyed, which was why, beside it, sat a Latin translation, and another note for Romanus himself, written in large print.

"Emperor Romanus, today, you may take my city, but I destroy your faith."

Kane/Lee Residence, Fairfax Towers

Falls Church, Virginia

Present Day

CIA Operations Officer Dylan Kane woke to a stabbing pain in his wrist. His CIA customized TAG Heuer watch was designed to give him an increasingly stronger electrical shock to gain his attention, and when he was asleep, it could get to ridiculous proportions, especially if he had been drinking.

Last night had gotten a little out of hand. It was just the usual group, himself, his girlfriend Lee Fang, his best friend Chris Leroux, and Leroux's girlfriend Sherrie White. It had been a while since the four of them had been able to get together, enjoy a nice meal, and tie one on without being interrupted by their jobs, three of the four employed by the CIA.

Now, with his head pounding and his stomach churning, he would have preferred the interruption to have happened last night, before the festivities kicked into high gear.

He rolled out of bed before pressing the button to end the torture, a lesson he had learned long ago. When in this state, he would too often press the button then fall back to sleep, only to be woken later with an even more powerful shock. He stretched then reached for his pre-positioned water bottle, draining half of it. He pressed the coded sequence around the watch face then frowned at the message projected on the crystal.

It was a message from Laura Palmer through his private communications network. She was the wife of his former archaeology professor from college. He respected them both tremendously, despite being a pain in his ass far too often. Yet they never contacted him unless it was absolutely necessary, and it was usually something he or his contacts could help with.

As much as he'd like to go back to sleep, he couldn't ignore it.

He logged into his secure messenger on his phone then frowned as he read the message. Acton was missing, possibly kidnapped in Istanbul by some Italian-based cult. Normally blame could be assigned quite easily, but Istanbul should be safe for a mild-mannered professor. As he continued to read the message, his frown deepened.

Okay, perhaps not so innocent.

The tablet was certainly a red flag. It could attract all manner of crazies, though apparently Leather's team was on the ground, only delayed in a manner that couldn't be coincidence. And why would they meet at the hotel and not the airport? That had to be Acton's idea, not Leather's.

"What's wrong?"

Kane glanced over his shoulder at the smolderingly hot former Chinese Special Forces operative he now shared a life with. "It looks like Jim Acton has been kidnapped in Istanbul."

"Again?"

He chuckled. "I don't think he's been kidnapped there before, but who knows."

"What are you going to do?"

"I'll get the gang on it, see if they can pull some footage. If he was kidnapped like Laura says, then we might be able to get a plate, perhaps track the vehicle."

"Well, good luck with that." Fang rolled back over and was asleep within seconds. She was tiny, and her tolerance for alcohol couldn't possibly match the gifted Sherrie, whom his love had attempted to match drink for drink.

Kane sent a message to Leroux, not expecting a response.

You up?

It went unanswered as he headed into the bathroom, sending an acknowledgment to Laura.

Message received. Will contact you when I find out something.

He received an immediate reply.

Thank you so much. Let me know of any funding requirements.

Acknowledged.

He stared at himself in the mirror, buck naked, and debated taking a quick shower. If this turned into something, it might be the last chance to freshen up, though if it did become something, he doubted he'd be directly involved on the ground. Not only was it nine or ten hours to

Istanbul, even with Laura's connections it would take a couple of hours to get a flight. Half a day was an eternity in a kidnapping. It would be Leroux's team that would handle things.

Assuming their boss approved.

He stared at his phone for a moment before sending a message to Leif Morrison, the CIA's National Clandestine Service chief.

You up?

The reply was almost immediate.

I shouldn't be.

Kane grinned.

Professor Acton has been kidnapped in Istanbul. Permission to activate Leroux's team?

There was a long pause that had him turning on the shower.

Granted. Observation only. No ground assets.

Kane smiled as he stepped into the shower.

Understood. Nighty-night.

Leroux/White Residence, Fairfax Towers

Falls Church, Virginia

"Wakey-wakey."

CIA Analyst Supervisor Chris Leroux bolted upright in bed, searching for the source of his wakeup call, but finding nothing. It took him a moment to remember he was wearing an eye mask, but someone else in bed was far more coordinated.

"Don't shoot, it's me."

It was Kane's voice, but even in his post-drinking stupor, he distinctly remembered his friend going back to his apartment when they were done. After all, they lived in the same building so couch-crashing wasn't necessary. Leroux ripped off his eye mask to see Kane standing at the foot of the bed, his hands up, while Leroux's girlfriend, CIA Operations Officer Sherrie White, pointed her gun squarely at him.

She lowered it. "My God, Dylan. Do you have a death wish?"

Kane shrugged as he lowered his hands. "I didn't think you were packing in bed." He grinned. "That's *his* job."

Leroux groaned as he rolled out of bed. "What the hell are you doing here at"—he glanced at the alarm clock—"four in the morning."

"We've got an op."

"What? We all clocked off. They shouldn't be calling us. We're all probably still drunk."

"That may be, but there's trouble in academia, and we've been called in."

Sherrie cursed. "Are you effing kidding me! What the hell did those two do now?"

Kane laughed. "It's just Jim. He's apparently been kidnapped in Istanbul, and the Chief has given us permission to get involved. Intel only, no ground assets."

Leroux's stomach churned and he raced for the bathroom, hurling last night's festivities into the toilet. He hated getting sick, and usually prided himself on rarely losing the battle. But this was just too soon, and the prospect of heading into the office to run an op was literally sickening. He rejoined the others. "I can't. I'm in no condition."

"Neither am I, which is why I'm handing it off to you."

Leroux gave his friend a look. "Sometimes you're an asshole."

Kane grinned. "That's the spirit! Look, we need an op center, and operatives can't run one of those. We need a pro, and that's you."

"Bullshit. I'm wasted."

Sherrie agreed. "He is. He just said 'wayshted.' Why don't you call Sonya? That poor girl has no social life. She'd probably jump at the opportunity to cover for you until you sober up."

It was a good idea. An excellent idea, though it was taking advantage of her social situation, or lack thereof. Not to mention the fact she was carrying a torch for him and would never refuse any request, even if she desperately wanted to.

"Fine, I'll call her. But next time, don't volunteer me for anything."

"I make no promises," said Kane.

Leroux stared at his friend. "Wait a minute, how did you get in."

Kane held up his keys. "You gave me a spare, remember?"

"I want it back."

Kane shook his head. "Do you really think a door lock can keep me out?"

Sherrie tapped her Glock. "No, but next time I'm shooting first, then seeing who it is."

Tong Residence

Falls Church, Virginia

CIA Senior Analyst Sonya Tong rolled over and grabbed her phone as it demanded her attention. She had it in Sleep Mode, so it had to be important—the only numbers she had programmed to let through at this hour were the most important people in her life, and those were few. Fewer still if you eliminated those who would never call at this hour.

The call display showed it was Leroux, which had her heart racing for multiple reasons. She chastised herself for the fleeting thought that he was calling to tell her he had dumped Sherrie and wanted to spend his life with her.

You're a fool.

She swiped her thumb on the display. "Hello?"

"Hi Sonya, it's Chris. I'm sorry to wake you at this hour, but we have an op."

She smiled slightly. He was loaded. She had never heard him drunk before, and it was impossibly cute how he struggled to sound sober. It just made it worse. "An op? What's it involve?"

"Dylan will be sending you all the details."

"Hey!" shouted Kane in the background.

"The op's been approved by the Chief. I'll be in as soon as I can—"

"He's shitfaced. He'll be in much later," said Sherrie, Tong's stomach twisting at the woman's voice.

She pushed through. "Okay, I'll notify the team and head in. We were scheduled off for the next two days so I can't guarantee everyone will be able to make it."

"All I need is you. You're the besht," replied Leroux, and her heart leaped at the words, her mind generating countless romantic alternatives to their true meaning.

"Thanks, boss. I'll take care of everything. You get your sleep and we'll see you in the morning."

"Okay. Good night. Don't let the bed bugs bite. I wonder what that means?"

Loud sounds came from the phone then Sherrie's voice replaced Leroux's. "He's useless now. He'll contact you in the morning, and Dylan will contact you shortly with all the details. Remember, this is *his* fault."

Tong chuckled. "Understood. Good night."

She ended the call then activated the app on her phone to initiate the snowball that would bring in the team before heading to the shower, fantasies continuing to dominate her thoughts.

All I need is you. You're the best.

Acton/Palmer Residence

St. Paul, Maryland

The hour was ridiculous, and Reading was operating on adrenaline alone. His best friend was missing, and his other best friend was on a flight heading into God knows what trouble. Tommy Granger, a computer phenom, and his girlfriend, Mai Trinh, one of Acton's staff at the university, were setting up several laptops and PCs on the dining table of his suite, the young couple answering Laura's desperate call immediately.

But he was fading fast, and there was nothing he could do to help until Tommy found something they could action. He had already sent a message to his partner at Interpol, Michelle Humphrey, and had received an acknowledgment that she would look into things. Other than that, he had done everything he could, but once things rolled, he would be much more involved.

"I'm going to bed. I need to get some rest before this gets going."

Mai smiled at him. "No problem. You get your sleep and we'll wake you if we find something we think you need to see."

Reading struggled to his feet and both Mai and Tommy rushed forward, each taking an arm. "Just get me my walker."

Mai grabbed it and brought it over. Reading gripped it tight then made his way to the bedroom.

"Need any help getting into bed?" asked Tommy.

"That'll be the day!" Reading closed the door and hobbled to his bed, out of breath. He was getting better, there was no doubt, but he was impatient. Incredibly impatient. He had to think of things in terms of weeks, not days. Day to day he didn't notice a difference, and some days he even felt like he had regressed, but if he thought of where he was a week ago, the progress had been tremendous.

He just had to keep his spirits up, and that was difficult with one friend in trouble, and the other heading into it.

He entered the bathroom and removed his clothes, the bandages hiding the scars he would be facing for the rest of his life. They would be a constant reminder of what that bastard had done to him, though he did take some satisfaction in knowing the piece of shit was dead, and that the children and the others had made it to safety.

A small price to pay?

He sighed. He had to convince himself of that sometimes, though considering he had gone into the situation with the expectation he would be killed, he should be thankful he had made it out alive, despite his weakened condition. A temporary state, if all the medical professionals were to be believed.

Yet he still had the nightmares, still woke up drenched in sweat, sometimes crying out as he relived the horrendous pain of the machete slicing open his chest. He closed his eyes and gripped the countertop, battling the tears. This wasn't him. This wasn't the man he knew he was. It took a lot to make him cry, but he had been weepy for weeks, and if he thought about it, months if not the past few years.

It was the heart problems.

The doctors had explained the blockage in his artery that was now fixed would have slowly drained him of energy, and that was probably why he had become more lethargic over the years, leading to weight gain and a loss of muscle mass.

And the damned desk I live behind at work.

He slapped his stomach, bigger than it had ever been, swearing to get rid of it when he was recovered. He was tired of feeling sorry for himself, and if it was his weakened heart that had been the root cause, then that excuse was gone. He would embrace his second chance, and live life to the fullest.

But first, he had to save his friend.

And get some sleep.

Hierapolis

AD 1068

Emperor Romanus IV Diogenes stared out a window of the headquarters of his defeated enemy, disappointed to find the man and his senior staff had somehow managed to escape. Word from captured soldiers loyal to the emir suggested there was an underground escape route that led out of the city. He had his men searching for it, for both ends, yet he had no doubt it was already too late.

The emir was gone, likely safely joining the troops gathering to the south, preparing for a counterattack.

It would fail.

The Roman Army was strong once again, and would only get stronger in the months and years ahead. This was their last campaign of the season. Winter would be setting in shortly, threatening their supply routes. It was time to fortify the city, leave behind a garrison strong enough to maintain control, then march north and return to Constantinople, where, by the time he arrived, his child would be born.

It had been wonderful news, and he prayed to God and the Lord Jesus Christ each night for a son, though should he have a daughter, he would be happy as well and prayed for her good health. He had sought the position he now occupied, though he had never thought he would attain it in the manner he had. His coup attempt had failed, he had been captured, arrested, charged, tried, and convicted.

And pardoned by the woman he now loved.

The woman whose sons he had sought to depose.

And who were now his stepchildren.

A remarkable turn of events, and a much more positive one than what he had in mind originally.

Now the challenge was the Doukai family. He had received a letter from the empress warning him of their scheming behind the scenes, and it outraged him, especially Caesar John's interaction with Michael.

It was unacceptable, and John would be spoken to.

Yet this was the political aspect of his new position. He was a soldier and sought power to protect the empire from its enemies, to restore the armies to their former glory, and to take the fight to those who threatened their borders, determined to take what Romans had built over a millennium.

More barbarians at the gates.

Rome had fallen six centuries ago, yet Rome lived on in Constantinople, and in its people. They were every bit as Roman as those who had come from the home of their ancestors. The great Emperor Constantine had established the new capital in his name, knowing the empire's future depended upon a secure location. He built a city with walls so great, it could never be sacked, and Rome, its values preserved by its people, would continue.

And he was determined to keep it that way. Once the armies were of sufficient size, he would take the fight farther to the south and east as he already planned, but he would also take it to the north and west, eventually retaking all former Roman territory. And when he was done, and after the empire was secure once again, returned to its former glory, he would happily step aside and allow Michael Doukas, his stepson, to assume the throne as full emperor, not just co-emperor.

The Doukai family would maintain their control of the throne, and peace would reign.

He was certain this would displease some in his family as he had no doubt once he had ascended, many saw brilliant futures for themselves and their children. Yet that was never his intention. He thought only of the empire, and what was best for it. Today, that was him, a strong military leader who would restore order. Tomorrow, when the job was done, it would require a firm administrator who would have learned what happens when the glorious Roman Army was left to wither on the vine.

It would be a magnificent future, certain to last another thousand years and beyond, perhaps one day encompassing the entire world. One people, under God, ruled from Constantinople, Pax Romana once again restored.

Peace, where warriors could lay down their weapons as they were needed no more.

It was a dream, perhaps ridiculous, and certainly not achievable in his lifetime nor that of his grandchildren, though perhaps eventually. But today, he had to secure this city before he could return home and welcome his new child into a proud family with an even prouder future.

He stared out the window of the citadel that had served as his enemy's headquarters, fires burning across the city, screams and cries of the enemy piercing the evening as his men executed those that lived. Tonight would be brutal for the people of Hierapolis, but tomorrow order would be restored, repairs would begin, and life would eventually return to normal for the citizenry, now under the protection and administration of the civilized Romans, and not the barbaric Arabs.

"Sir, you have to see this!" hissed Alexander, his trusted advisor and best friend for many years.

Romanus turned to find him standing in the doorway, his face pale, his eyes wide. He couldn't recall ever seeing fear on the man's face, but if this was it, he must have found something truly disturbing, for there was no evidence of any threat nearby. "What is it?"

"I...I'm not sure. You must see it. We found it in the emir's office, on his desk." Alexander beckoned him to follow, and moments later they were in the office of his defeated foe, half a dozen of his soldiers standing around the large desk at the far end. They snapped to attention and Alexander flicked his wrist. "Everybody out." He raised a finger before they could move. "And it's your head if anyone mentions what was found here today." He lowered the finger and the men hurried out, leaving them alone. He gestured toward the desk. "There was a note left for you, and...something else."

Romanus' curiosity was piqued to say the least, and he still wasn't certain what had his friend so on edge to the point where he would threaten the lives of his own men should they talk of what he had yet to see. He stepped over to the desk and picked up the note, his eyebrows rising as he read it aloud.

"Today, you may take my city, but I destroy your faith." He shook the page, turning to Alexander. "What in the name of God does that mean?"

Alexander shifted uncomfortably. "There's more."

Romanus flipped the page over, finding it blank.

"No, sir, on the desk. There's a tablet. It appears to be written in Hebrew, and there's a translation."

Romanus pursed his lips and stepped around the desk, spotting what appeared to be a stone tablet, the language of the Jews carved into its surface. He had seen the language on several occasions, but it was rare. The tablet must be very old, not only because of the language used, but the fact stone had been used instead of paper. It was clearly something meant to last through the ages.

He noticed the translation beside it, written in Latin, and as he read it, his skin crawled and his stomach churned. He collapsed into the chair behind the desk as all strength left him. He stared up at his friend. "This…this can't be true!"

Alexander glanced nervously behind him, making certain they were still alone, though still stepped closer and lowered his voice. "But…but what if it is?"

Romanus shook his head. "I don't know. If it is, if it is true, it changes everything." He drew a breath and held it for a moment before exhaling loudly, repeating this several times as the strength slowly returned to his body. He pointed at the tablet. "There is a location here. We must go there as soon as possible."

Alexander shook his head. "We can't. It's too far south, well into enemy territory, and the campaigning season is over. We must return to Constantinople."

Romanus grabbed at his temples, squeezing them with one hand as he closed his eyes. This was simply too much. If it were true, everything they had been taught for nearly a millennium was a lie. The Bible was a lie.

And the Son of God was just a man.

No better or worse than anyone else of the day.

He had to know the truth.

He rose and pointed at the tablet. "Take that and the translation with you, and never let it out of your personal possession. When we return to Constantinople, we will consult the clergy."

"Yes, sir."

Romanus headed for the door then stopped, turning back to his friend. "And one more thing."

"Sir?"

"Kill anyone who saw this. If word gets out, the very Church could be destroyed."

Operations Center 3, CIA Headquarters

Langley, Virginia

Present Day

Sonya Tong entered the state-of-the-art operations center buried in the bowels of CIA Headquarters and yawned. It was too early on a Saturday morning for her. Just a few more hours and she would have been fine to come in, but unfortunately that wasn't in the cards apparently. Friday nights for her were just more of the same boring. Nobody had gone for drinks after work for some reason, so she had gone home, ordered a pizza, then binged Ozark while nursing a bottle of chardonnay. Not enough to get drunk, just enough to be comfortably numb.

It was a lonely life. She had debated getting a dog or a cat, but she never had a pet as a child, and she wasn't sure she wanted to make the commitment now. And besides, it might shut down her chance at happiness in the future. What if she met someone but they didn't like cats or dogs?

Analyst Supervisor Avril Casey, the temporary coordinator who kept the place warm with a skeleton team, smiled at her, the beautiful woman probably someone who had an active social life. "So, you're the poor sap who gets to set things up?"

Tong shrugged. "I made the mistake of being sober."

Casey laughed. "You should have accepted Chris' offer to join them."

Tong paused. "He never invited me."

"Yes, he did. In the breakroom. I heard him and you made some lame excuse about not wanting to be a fifth wheel. He's too nice a guy to press, so he let it go." Casey leaned closer and lowered her voice. "If the fifth wheel wants to meet a sixth, she has to get out there a little more."

Tong flushed. "Yeah, I suppose so." She indicated the massive displays wrapping across the front of the room. "You got the briefing from Kane, I see."

"Yes. Lots of typos. I assume he's hammered?"

"They all are. What have you got so far?"

Casey nodded toward the screen. "We have footage of Professor Acton getting off the plane, entering the terminal, then getting into an SUV escorted by a chauffeur."

"Where did they go?"

"Still tracking that, but so far everything looks completely innocent."

"Except for the fact no chauffeur was sent."

"Correct."

"His cellphone?"

"No trace of it yet. It suggests that either the chauffeur or the SUV has a jammer."

"Which means this isn't just a mix-up. Okay, let me get set up then I'll formally relieve you. A few of the team have confirmed they're on the way. I think, however, I'm going to need most of your team until their shift ends."

"No problem, we live to serve." A round of exaggeratedly depressed yays erupted from the team and Tong laughed as Casey dismissed it with a batted hand. "Behave!"

Tong headed for her traditional station when one of the team caught everyone's attention.

"Found it!"

Casey turned. "Found what where?"

"The SUV." The woman pointed at the screen and footage appeared showing an SUV being towed. "Looks like it broke down."

Casey grunted. "That makes sense. Look what make it is."

Tong wasn't as convinced. "I doubt it. I'm guessing it was abandoned. Let's trace that back, see where they picked it up, then look for any unusual activity. They had to know they would be traced, so my guess is they switched vehicles."

Casey faced her team. "See, people, that's day-shift thinking."

And her team began a well-rehearsed chant. "We suck! We suck!"

Dig Site

Kınalıada Island, Turkey

Professor Boran looked up as someone called his name. He peered into the sunlight and it wasn't until he shielded his eyes that he recognized who had hailed him. "Professor Acton?"

Acton smiled broadly as he approached. "Please, call me Jim."

Boran stood in shock, as did everyone else, the entire team well aware that this man was apparently kidnapped earlier in the day. "Forgive me for being indelicate, Jim, but where the hell have you been? You realize everyone is looking for you?"

Acton laughed. "Yeah, I'm sorry about that. Just a misunderstanding." He extended a hand and Boran shook it. "I hope I didn't put you out."

Boran shrugged. "No, just a few phone calls and a lot of worry. Have you contacted your wife? She was desperate to reach you, as were several others including your security team."

Acton glanced about. "Are they here?"

"Your team was, but once they confirmed you weren't, they left. Their priority was you, not the site."

"But you have hired your own security?"

"Yes. We have six armed guards on rotating shifts, thanks to your generous donation."

"Happy to hear it. Now, how about you give me that tour you've been promising and we see this tablet that has everyone so excited."

"Everyone? Has word gotten out? I had my people delete everything they had posted."

Acton chuckled as they headed inside. "No, I meant you, me, my wife, your team."

"Oh. Well, you're going to love this."

Boran gave him a thorough tour of the grounds, then the chamber where the sarcophagus had been discovered. He was impressed with Acton's knowledge, his questions on point and intelligent, though he had a sense the man was impatient. He would be too, he supposed, if he knew what the tour culminated in, though he had a feeling it wasn't for that reason.

Where had the man been? He had been gone for almost two hours, then showed up with no explanation other than it was a misunderstanding. A misunderstanding? What did that even mean? A dead cellphone, a screwed-up reservation, a delay, those were all perfectly good explanations, but they weren't misunderstandings.

Something wasn't right.

Unfortunately, he couldn't interrogate the man since he was funding the dig. He had to accept that his questions would go unanswered.

"Are you ready to see the pièce de résistance?"

Acton grinned. "Am I!"

"In anticipation of your arrival, I had it brought back from our vault at the university. I figured with the security team, it was safe to do so."

"I'm sure you're right."

He led him into another room off the main chamber, empty save a table and several high-powered lights illuminating its surface. Some of his team were examining the find, taking additional photographs, and they paused their work.

"I'd like to view it in private, please."

"Of course." Boran flicked his wrist and his team scrambled out of the room. "Do you want me to leave?"

Acton shook his head. "No, of course not." He rushed forward, circling the table as his expert eye took in every detail. He pulled a magnifying glass from his well-worn leather satchel and leaned in for a closer examination. "Have you been able to determine anything?"

"Not really. Carbon dating on the remains is consistent with the era, but of course the stone itself can't be dated. Our experts tell us the Biblical Hebrew it was written in is accurate to the era of when Jesus Christ was thought to have existed."

"And the writing itself. There's no indication it was done around the time of the burial?"

Boran paused. "I'm not sure how we would determine that."

"Shavings. Did you find any stray shavings in the sarcophagus or on the surface of the tablet? If it was a thousand years old at the time of its burial, there would be none. If it had been carved a week before, there might be."

Boran's eyebrows shot up. "I hadn't thought of that. But no, we found nothing of the sort, and believe me, we've been through that sarcophagus with a literal fine-toothed comb."

"Good. Of course, if it were fake, a skilled craftsman would have thoroughly brushed it down and aged it, making certain no one would find any evidence of his handiwork."

Boran pursed his lips. "So, you think it's a fake?"

"I hope it's a fake, but to what end? Why would someone in the eleventh century create this? Or, if it does date from the time of Christ, why would someone create it then? What this claims is so shocking, it could cause the very troubles we've been worried about. But back then? Romanus could have simply destroyed it. And even if it were proven to be true, would those who proved it share that truth with the world, or go to their graves hiding it? But if it is indeed from the time of Christ's crucifixion, then why create this for any other purpose than to record the truth."

"So then, you believe it could be genuine."

Acton sighed. "If we could only know when it was created. If it's eleventh century, then obviously it's a fraud. If it's first century, then I see no reason why anyone would write a forgery such as this. Christianity wasn't a thing back then, so why would you chisel a tablet with this lie?"

Boran tensed. "My God. Romanus had to believe it was real, otherwise he wouldn't have had it buried with him. He had to have had some reason to believe it could be true."

"It would certainly explain why a brilliant soldier and tactician made so many errors in his final campaigns. He kept trying to take land to the south before his armies were prepared." Acton stabbed a finger toward the tablet. "That has to be the reason why. He was determined to reach the location indicated so he could prove the truth one way or the other."

"But he failed." Boran shuddered. "He obviously feared it was true, otherwise he would have smashed it where he found it."

"I'm not sure of his motivations, but I'm sure of one thing. In today's world, with modern communications and a twisted social media, this will be used to foment hate. We have to determine the truth, one way or the other, then decide what to do."

"How are we going to do that?"

"I'm going to Syria."

Boran's eyes shot wide. "Syria? Are you out of your mind? I've mapped where that location is. It's in the heart of the conflict. It's not safe. And there's no way they'll let an archaeology team in there. There's no way we'll ever get permission."

Acton squinted at the wall. "What's that?"

Boran turned and saw nothing, but before he could ask what he should be looking for, Acton came up from behind him and grabbed him around the neck, placing him in a chokehold. "What...are you...doing?" he gasped, struggling against the iron grip, but it was no use.

"I'm sorry, Deniz. When this is all over, I'll explain everything."

They were the last words he was to hear as this man he had never met choked the life out of him, and his world fell black.

Park Hyatt Istanbul Macka Palas

Istanbul, Turkey

Cameron Leather sent the hourly update to Reading. Tommy Granger had managed to hack the Istanbul Ataturk Airport camera feeds and they had footage of Acton getting into an SUV outside the private charter terminal with a chauffeur. Tommy was attempting to track the vehicle, but Leather had little doubt they would have switched cars by now.

Not meeting Acton at the airport was a tactical mistake. The concern, however, had never been his clients' safety, it was the danger the find at the archaeological dig site could put them in when they got there. Few should have known that Acton was coming, and the crazies they were worried about when the plans were made shouldn't be targeting the professors specifically.

All that changed, of course, when he was informed the Keepers of the One Truth could be involved. From what he had been told about them by the professors, they were dangerous. Very dangerous. They weren't a cult that set out to kill simply for killing's sake. After all, they were very religious, not suffering from the fundamentalist belief that all who disagreed with them must die. But their oath to protect the Church from anything that might harm it meant if one got in their way, one's life could be in danger.

When he had found out, they were already on the plane for Istanbul from Cairo, originally scheduled to arrive just before him where they would then establish a base of operations at the hotel in preparation for his arrival. Instead, they had been delayed leaving Cairo, just long enough for them to arrive about half an hour after his client.

And that was too much of a coincidence.

It meant that the Keepers had connections not only in the Vatican, but also in Rome, Istanbul, and Cairo.

They were too well connected to take on easily.

Now his focus was to find Acton and get him back home safely. Unfortunately, his other client, Laura Palmer, was on her way here. He had already said she shouldn't come, but there was no reasoning with the woman when it came to her husband.

He admired their devotion to each other, and their commitment to their students. They were the best clients he could have asked for, and they paid ridiculously well. He had started his security firm when he left the SAS, bringing in Spec Ops soldiers from various countries over the years, giving former warriors a stable income surrounded by people who knew what they had been through, and who had their backs when necessary.

They were a family, and he loved it.

He leaned back in his chair and folded his arms. "Why would they kidnap him?"

Warren Reese, one of his longest-serving team members, shrugged. "Like the warning said. 'Do not interfere.' I guess they thought he'd interfere."

"But why kidnap him? They could have just shot him, or with their connections, had him detained at the airport. If they were able to jam his cellphone signal on the tarmac and in the terminal, then that means they could have planted anything they wanted in his luggage. They could have had him in a Turkish prison by lunch. He'd be out of their way for days if not years."

Reese chewed his cheek. "Maybe they wanted to know what he knows."

Leather's head bobbed. "Interrogate him first. But then what?"

"Hold him until they're done? Kill him and dump the body somewhere it would never be found?"

"Or use him."

They both turned toward Ashton Schmidt, their tech expert, who swung his laptop around, an image of Acton shown shaking a man's hand.

"What am I looking at?" asked Leather.

"You wanted me to monitor the social media accounts of the dig team. One of them just posted this five minutes ago."

Leather paused, confused. "Wait. Are you saying Acton is at the dig site?"

"Unless this has been photoshopped, then yes."

He dialed Acton's number and it still went directly to voicemail.

What the hell is going on here?

Dig Site

Kınalıada Island, Turkey

Acton lay Boran gently onto the floor then checked the man's pulse to make sure he hadn't taken the sleeper hold too far. Boran would be fine and awake in minutes, so he had little time to act. He pulled out the phone his captors had provided him, his own confiscated, and sent a message.

I'm on my way.

He pulled a large cloth from his satchel then carefully wrapped the tablet, placing it inside his bag. He drew a deep breath then strode from the room. He smiled at one of Boran's team members. "Professor Boran has asked not to be disturbed for the next ten minutes."

"Yes, sir. I'll make sure he's left alone."

Acton headed outside and into the afternoon sunlight. He walked with purpose the same way he had come in, his heart pounding at what he had done. He had assaulted an innocent man. He had stolen an ancient artifact. He was a criminal. He could be arrested and thrown into a Turkish prison for years.

Yet he had no choice.

If he hadn't done what he had, the Keepers would kill Laura. He had no reason to doubt them after seeing them in action before. They were ruthless and would show no mercy toward anyone who got in their way. He had to make it out of here undiscovered, then the next step was in his blackmailers' hands.

He climbed the steps to the upper road that ran across the north side of the dig, acknowledging two of the armed guards. He kept a brisk though controlled pace as he headed toward the pier, the boat that had brought him here now in sight.

A cry behind him had his heart leaping into his throat, the urge to run overwhelming. He kept his pace steady as shouts erupted, then a whistle blew repeatedly, a poor man's alarm if he ever heard one.

And surprisingly effective.

The engine on the boat sprang to life, exhaust erupting in a burst, but he kept his pace. Something was shouted behind him in Turkish. It wasn't from the dig site, but from the road. It had to be one of the guards ordering him to stop.

"Halt!"

Sometimes he hated being right.

He continued on, maintaining his pace when footfalls behind him changed the plan. He sprinted toward the boat and a shot rang out behind him. He ducked but kept going. He had to deliver the tablet to the Keepers. He had no choice. He'd throw it on the boat if he had to, he didn't care. His life was forfeit if it meant saving Laura's. Another shot and the gravel ahead of him erupted in a puff, the bullets now aimed at him, the warning shot apparently the only one.

He lifted the strap for his satchel off his shoulder as his feet hit the wooden pier. The boat was at the far end, still idling, still waiting for him. Another shot rang out and he prepared to hurl the bag when two Keepers emerged from the hold carrying AK-47s. They sprayed bullets over his head and he glanced over his shoulder, praying none of his pursuers had been shot.

He didn't want an accessory to murder charge added to his list of crimes.

Thankfully, the guards had hit the ground, scrambling out of the line of fire. Acton leaped onto the boat and the engine gunned, sending him tumbling to the deck. They pulled rapidly away from the pier as the two gunmen fired several more bursts, keeping his pursuers at bay, and within moments they were safely into the Sea of Marmara.

The leader stepped out of the deckhouse. "Did you get it?"

Acton held up the satchel. "Yes."

"Good. Now we go to Syria."

Acton frowned. "And then we die."

Great Palace of Constantinople

Constantinople, Eastern Roman Empire

AD 1069

"He's dead," hissed Alexander as he closed the inner door of Romanus' private offices in the palace. Romanus glanced up from the pile of papers the administration of an empire necessitated, and recognized the fear on his friend's face, a fear he had only seen once before.

In Hierapolis, when they had found the mysterious tablet.

"Who is dead?"

"The bishop."

Romanus leaned back in his chair, eying his friend, still not making the connection. "Which—" Then he realized what Alexander was talking about. "Wait, you mean Bishop Ignatius?"

Alexander rapidly nodded as he approached. "Yes. I showed him the tablet and the translation, as you asked me to. He read it, and it was clear he was disturbed. He called in several advisors, one of who reads Hebrew, and he confirmed the translation as accurate."

Romanus pinched the bridge of his nose, the stress of the position getting to him. He far preferred directing men on the battlefield than pushing paper around his desk. "But is it genuine? We have a Latin translation of a Hebrew tablet. Did you ever doubt that the translation wasn't accurate?"

Alexander paused then shrugged. "I had hoped, I suppose."

"Of course you hoped, we both hoped, but you knew as well as I did that they would match. That wasn't the question we needed answered. We needed to know whether the tablet itself was genuine. Was it carved a thousand years ago like it claims, or last week by our enemy, attempting to shake our faith?"

"Well, if the bishop thought it was fake, he wouldn't have killed himself now, would he?"

"What happened?"

"He shouted something from the balcony, slit his throat, and tumbled to the ground."

Romanus slumped in his chair, stunned. For the bishop to kill himself over what was written on the tablet could mean only one thing. He believed it was genuine. Romanus' skin crawled as it had the day they discovered the tablet in Hierapolis. If it were true, it would destroy Christianity. It meant most of the New Testament was a lie, and the entire Church was built on a fiction. The founding tenets of the Church were false, and the entirety of the Roman Empire and beyond that worshipped Jesus Christ had been lied to for a millennium.

He tilted his head forward and pinched the bridge of his nose again. Hard. He needed the pain to bring him some sense. He needed to know the truth. And one clergyman killing himself over what he had read was not proof.

It made no sense.

"Do we know what he shouted?"

Alexander shook his head. "I'm afraid not. Nobody was close enough to hear what he said."

"How much time did he spend with the tablet?"

"I believe in total I was there a few hours before he…"

"And all he did was read the translation, bring in someone who reads Hebrew to confirm its accuracy, then killed himself."

"Well, there was some discussion among the senior clergy that lasted at least an hour, then he excused himself, and the next thing I knew, he was on the ground below."

"Was there any discussion on whether the tablet was genuine?"

"I'm certain there was, though I think they were more concerned with the words and their meaning."

"I think their meaning is quite clear."

"Yes, of course. I suppose I should have said, their implications."

Romanus leaned back, shaking his head slowly. "Yes, the implications. We are still faced with the problem this tablet represents."

Alexander stepped closer, lowering his voice. "Why don't we simply destroy it?"

Romanus regarded his friend. It was one possible solution to the harm that could come should the tablet's contents be made public, but there was another problem. The truth had to be known. Had they all been lied to for a thousand years? Had it all been a hoax? The tablet had a location on it, and he had to reach that location to prove whether Christianity was the greatest hoax perpetrated by man, against man.

Were twelve disciples simply followers of a carpenter with charisma?

And that carpenter wasn't the Son of God at all.

He looked at his friend. "No. The truth must be known. If we can prove that the location doesn't exist, that there is nothing there, then we can discard the tablet for the blasphemy it is. But if it is true, then we must know."

"And if it is true? Are you willing to reveal the truth to the people? To destroy their very belief system? To destroy the Holy Trinity? It would mean chaos! There would be rioting in the streets. The churches would be set aflame, the clergy massacred. Even your right to occupy the position of emperor could be challenged. It is too risky!"

"But what if it is true? Should we allow the people to continue to worship a fraud?"

"Why not? Better a fraud than the insane beliefs of the Jews or Arabs, or worse the pagans. If Jesus was a fraud, it doesn't mean God was. The Ten Commandments still apply. What Jesus taught is still good. Even if he was just a man, the words are still words to live by."

"Are they? We live by them because they were spoken by the Son of God. If they weren't, even if the words spoken were good, are they the best? Perhaps there are better words to live by, better ways to live our lives."

Alexander stared at him, wide-eyed. "Do you really doubt your faith so much, that you believe these words you speak?"

Romanus sighed, shaking his head. "No, of course not. At least, not yet. But this has raised doubts in me. If we are defenders of the faith, if we fight on the side of God and his Son, Jesus Christ, then why do we lose battles to heathens, to Arabs? Why do we suffer rebellions and plagues, droughts and famine? Shouldn't God be blessing us for fighting in his name, and inflicting defeat and suffering on our enemies who do not? If God is on our side, then who the hell is on the side of our enemies that we can be defeated?"

Alexander eyed him, his mouth agape. "What are you saying?"

"I'm saying that the Roman Empire was at its greatest when we worshipped Jupiter and the other gods. It wasn't until we embraced the beliefs of the Christians that we began to falter. Perhaps we back the wrong gods."

Alexander checked over both shoulders, confirming they were alone. "That's blasphemy!" he hissed. "They'll behead you for saying such things."

"It's only blasphemy if it isn't true."

"Surely you can't believe it is."

Romanus frowned. "I'm afraid I have my doubts." He rose, striding over to a large map that laid out the plans for his upcoming campaign. He pointed at a location to the south. "This is where the tablet suggests the truth is hidden. We must reach there as quickly as possible if we are to determine the truth and restore my faith, and preserve the faith of the people."

Alexander stood beside him, chewing his cheek. "This year's plans don't even come close. It would take two, perhaps three years."

"Agreed. We will have to modify them. The truth can't wait that long."

"But we risk defeat. We could lose everything."

"If all we have been fighting for, if all we have believed for so long is a lie, then we have already lost everything worth losing."

Approaching Kınalıada Island, Turkey

Present Day

"Bloody hell!"

Leather had to agree with the sentiment expressed by Reese. As they approached the pier adjacent to the dig site, he ordered the pilot to slow to a crawl. He wanted time to assess the situation before docking. The island was crawling with police. Something had obviously gone down here, and it wasn't good.

He just prayed it was the theft they had worried about, rather than the attack they had feared.

"All right, everyone remain calm. Reese, you'll come with me. Everyone else stay on the boat. We don't want the locals getting too nervous." He turned to their local contact, Irmak. "I'll let you do the talking. All I want to know is what happened, and where Professor Acton is."

"Understood." Irmak disappeared inside the cabin for a moment then returned, sans weapons. He was fully licensed, however there was no danger here except from on-edge police.

They pulled up to the pier and two of the crew tied the rental off as Irmak disembarked, immediately challenged by several police, all sporting automatic weapons. A quick conversation took place then Irmak motioned for Leather to join him.

"Just hold back," said Leather to Reese before stepping onto the pier. He joined Irmak and smiled at the man he had been talking to.

"Captain Demirel, this is retired Lt. Colonel Cameron Leather, former British SAS. He's the head of security for Professors Acton and Palmer, who are the primary funders for this dig site through their foundation."

Leather extended his hand. "A pleasure, Captain."

Demirel shook his hand. "Likewise, Colonel. So, do you care to tell me what happened here today?"

Leather shook his head. "I'm sorry, Captain, but you have me at a disadvantage. When we arrived in Istanbul several hours ago, one of our clients, Professor Acton, was reported kidnapped."

"Kidnapped?"

"Yes. He was picked up at the airport by a chauffeur driving an SUV. The original plan was for him to rent a vehicle, and according to our contacts at the university, no chauffeur had been sent."

"But you are here, so obviously you knew something happened."

"I'm sorry again, Captain, but no." Leather pulled out his cellphone and showed the image of Acton at the site. "We found this on social media a short while ago while at our hotel. We immediately came here to find out what he was doing here. We haven't been able to reach him by phone, so we wanted to confirm he was safe. When we arrived, we saw all this."

Demirel pursed his lips, regarding him for several moments as he no doubt debated whether what he had been told was a load of bullshit. "Your story matches with what the university personnel here have told me, except in one important way."

Leather tensed. "What?"

"Professor Acton showed up here less than half an hour ago, assaulted Professor Boran, and stole a valuable artifact before boarding a boat that had at least two gunmen on it firing assault rifles."

Leather's eyebrows shot up. "Bloody hell. I can honestly say I wasn't expecting that. What artifact?" He knew the answer yet had to confirm it.

"Some tablet they aren't yet convinced is genuine."

"I see. And is Professor Boran all right?"

"He is. He was put into a chokehold and was unconscious for less than five minutes. We're still treating it as a failed homicide attempt, however."

"Why would you do that?"

"Because he could have killed him."

Leather shook his head. "If he wanted him dead, he'd be dead."

"What makes you say that?"

"I trained him. He knows exactly how to execute what would have been a sleeper hold. He rendered the professor unconscious so he could take the tablet. There was never any risk to Professor Boran, I can assure you."

Demirel eyed him. "Why would you teach him that?"

"My clients work in dangerous locations and have encountered a lot of dangerous people. The best way to keep them alive is to teach them how to keep themselves safe. I have trained them in hand-to-hand combat, weapons, tactics, hostage negotiations. Whatever it takes to survive the next minute."

"I hope you taught him how to survive in a prison, because that's where he's heading."

"Captain, I guarantee you that when this is all over, he'll have a perfectly good explanation for what happened here today."

"What happened here was attempted murder, theft, and assault with a deadly weapon."

"Yes, I can see how you might think that, but I'll ask you one question, Captain."

"What?"

"If Professor Acton is the bad guy here, then why didn't he have a gun?"

"What?"

"Why didn't he have a gun? If his so-called accomplices had assault rifles, and he was in on it, why didn't he at least have a handgun? He could have shot Professor Boran, shot the guards, held someone hostage while he made his escape. There are countless possibilities. Instead, he used his hands to expertly render someone unconscious, took the tablet, then got on a boat with armed gunmen. You know what that sounds like to me?"

Demirel frowned. "What?"

"Coercion. He was forced to do what he did by unknown forces."

"And just who are these unknown forces?"

Leather knew precisely who they were yet couldn't reveal the truth—it would simply be rejected as nonsense. "Likely the same people security was hired to protect against. Some fundamentalist group that found out about the tablet and wanted it for themselves."

Demirel eyed him for a moment. "What's so important about this tablet?"

Leather shrugged, deciding it wasn't his place to reveal the truth. "I don't know. I'm just here to provide security. I'm sure Professor Boran could tell you."

"He tells me it's something that could destroy Christianity."

"Then if that's true, don't you think every fundamentalist in the world would do anything they could to get their hands on it, including kidnapping my client? They could have discovered he was on his way here and given him orders to steal it, otherwise harm might come to him or those he cared about."

Demirel's head slowly bobbed. "An interesting theory, and it will be investigated. In the meantime, however, your client is wanted for the aforementioned charges, and will be put before the court unless I'm satisfied he was acting against his will."

Leather bowed slightly. "I would expect nothing less, and I appreciate the fact you are at least entertaining the possibility that he is innocent."

Demirel indicated the boat they had arrived on. "Give your contact information to my deputy, then get off my crime scene."

"Yes, Captain."

Acton/Palmer Residence

St. Paul, Maryland

Reading ended the call, his sleep interrupted by the update from Leather. He held up a finger, cutting off any questions from Tommy and Mai, and leaned back in his chair as he calmed his hammering heart. Acton was clearly being coerced into working for the Keepers of the One Truth or some other group. All evidence pointed to the Keepers, and for them to have let him out of their sight meant they were holding something over him.

Probably Laura's life.

Acton would do anything for her, even die for her, though he wouldn't kill innocents. They would both draw the line there. Yet as Leather had described it, no lives had been lost, Acton had expertly taken down Boran, and it was those on the boat who had fired at the guards, thankfully missing them. If it were the Keepers, they were well trained from what he had seen, which suggested they hadn't attempted to kill the guards. It was more likely they were warning shots.

122

Nobody was meant to die.

And they were on a small island, so letting Acton go in alone wasn't much of a risk for them, since he had nowhere to go.

He flicked a finger and the barrage began.

"Why do you think he did it?" asked Tommy, beating Mai to the punch.

"I'm guessing he was forced to by the Keepers."

It was Mai's turn. "Do you think they threatened Laura?"

"Yes."

"Shouldn't we stop her from going to Istanbul?"

Reading checked his watch. "When is she due to arrive?"

Tommy glanced at his tablet. "In three hours."

"She'd never agree. All we can do is update her, then let her decide. But we'll make sure Cam is at the airport with his team to meet her. The last thing we need is her getting kidnapped too. Right now, Jim is operating under the assumption she is safe, and will remain that way because of our actions."

"What do we do now?"

"We update Laura, get Cameron in position, and try to find any footage that shows where that boat Jim got on docked. We need to figure out where he is before he gets to where he's going."

Mai's eyes narrowed. "Where is he going?"

"If what I think is going on actually is, he's heading to Syria before the day is out."

Operations Center 3, CIA Headquarters
Langley, Virginia

Tong read the update from Reading and Leather, all declassified updates going into a shared secure folder. Things had escalated dramatically in the last thirty minutes, and if Leroux wasn't careful, he'd miss out on the action if he didn't sober up soon. She agreed with Reading's assessment that Acton's next most likely destination was the location on the tablet, and that was in modern-day Syria, one of the most dangerous places on the planet right now.

What she hadn't told them, though she had no doubt with Reading's law enforcement experience he already suspected, the Turkish police had put out the equivalent to an all-points bulletin on Acton, indicating he was wanted on numerous accounts, including terrorism. It was the terrorism charge that had her concerned. It was unwarranted, issued only to annoy the United States in the ongoing tit-for-tat bickering of the two official NATO allies.

She suspected that if it weren't for Turkey's geographical location, they would have been kicked out years ago after Erdogan solidified his power. It was a joke to have a country like that in NATO, but since the Bosporus Strait passed directly through Istanbul, joining the Black Sea ultimately to the Mediterranean, it was too important a strategic location to leave in the hands of Russia or China.

But geopolitics wasn't her concern, it was finding Acton before things got too far out of hand. He was obviously under the control of the Keepers of the One Truth, her briefing notes on the organization providing her with little beyond conjecture, but they were real, nonetheless. Whether she believed their backstory was irrelevant.

"I've got him getting off the boat," reported their tech wunderkind, Randy Child, who had arrived a few minutes ago reeking of garlic donair with his two days of growth peppered with Cheetos crumbs.

"Show me."

Footage appeared on the main display showing a boat pulling up to a dock and Acton getting off with four other men. None appeared armed, though they wore long robes that could conceal anything. More likely, however, they had left the weapons behind as they were no longer needed. The point now was to blend until they could get out of sight, not enter into a firefight with the local authorities because some citizen spotted the butt of a rifle.

"Track them. Let's see where they go."

"Should we notify the Turks?"

Tong chewed her cheek for a moment. If they did, and the Turks wanted them on terrorism charges, they'd go in shooting and Acton would likely be killed. This needed something more subtle.

"No, but get me Leather."

En route to the Park Hyatt Istanbul

Istanbul, Turkey

Leather swiped his thumb, taking the call from the unknown number as they drove back to their hotel. "Hello?"

"Hello, Colonel Leather, this is Sonya. Do you know who I am?"

He smiled slightly. He loved dealing with spy agencies. "Yes."

"Good. I've uploaded coordinates into the secure folder for where we last spotted Professor Acton. He got off a boat with four men, and they may or may not be armed."

Leather grabbed the tablet off the seat beside him then logged in, bringing up the folder. "Have you informed the locals?"

"Negative. I have concerns they may shoot first, ask questions later."

"Good thinking." He brought up the coordinates then sent them to the mapping app. He handed the tablet forward. "Get us there ASAP." A U-turn was abruptly executed resulting in curses from the passengers and protesting horns from those sharing the road with them.

"We're on our way. ETA…"

"Fifteen minutes," filled in the driver.

"Fifteen minutes. I assume you're still attempting to track him?"

"Yes. We'll continue feeding updates to the folder as we locate him, along with any images or footage. Be careful, Colonel, these people are dangerous."

"I'm always careful."

Istanbul, Turkey

Acton strode quickly, flanked by his four captors. They had dumped their AK-47s in the middle of the Sea of Marmara, though he had little doubt they still were packing handguns. He was confident he could make a break for it, but if they were armed, they'd simply shoot him in the back. In reality, they no longer needed him. He had retrieved the tablet with little difficulty, and now, despite their plans to go to Syria, they could kidnap someone else to guide them to the location. Only he could have retrieved the tablet, but any number of people could lead them to their destination.

He had to be careful. For the moment, they seemed content to keep him with them. If they wanted to part ways, they could have killed him, or simply left him behind in the boat, tied up. But they had taken him with them, and so far, other than the kidnapping and interrogation, had treated him reasonably well.

They walked through the crowded streets, and it gave him an opportunity to think. By now, the authorities had been notified and they

129

would no doubt assume he was involved. His photo was probably on every police officer's phone, and with his 'accomplices' likely not caught on camera, he'd be treated as the ringleader since they would have his full bio, no doubt eagerly provided by Boran.

He felt guilty about what he had done to the poor man. Not only was it a violent act, but it was never a good feeling to be bested by another man you considered an equal. He could have explained what was going on, but he couldn't count on Boran's cooperation. And there hadn't been time. The Keepers had told him he had only thirty minutes to retrieve the tablet or they would leave and kill Laura at some point in the future.

He believed them.

The tour had been excruciatingly long, though far shorter than he likely imagined. The escape had been terrifying, but it was over. Everyone was alive, nobody had been permanently hurt, and nothing had been damaged.

The question was, what now?

He already knew Reading and the others were involved based on what Boran had said. Leather was already in the city, and Acton had little doubt the man's team was already searching for him. If he knew Reading, he'd have reached out to his Interpol colleagues, and someone would have contacted Kane to see if their CIA friends could help.

Things were in motion to save him, but did he want to be saved?

Even if he were rescued from these four men, even if these four men were captured or killed, there were other Keepers spread around the world. They could kill Laura tomorrow as they left Istanbul, or next year while she shopped for groceries. This situation had to be resolved to the satisfaction of the Keepers, not himself. And then there was the fact he was dying to know the truth as well.

He could see no other choice. He had to not only cooperate with them but embrace the mission. He had to work with them so they could succeed in discovering the truth together, and while doing so, get them to trust him. He had to know what their endgame was. What would it take for them to release him, satisfied that he had done what they expected so Laura was safe?

They stepped into one of the dozens of cafés they had passed, and he was led to a table deep inside and away from prying eyes. They all sat and Turkish coffees were ordered. They waited in silence until their drinks were delivered and the waiter had left.

Acton decided it was time to see where he stood. "I need to know what you expect of me."

"Your cooperation," replied the leader.

"And you have it." Acton leaned forward, lowering his voice slightly. "Listen, we have the tablet, and no one was hurt. Stage one, complete. Now we're heading into Syria to find out if what this stone says is true. I don't have a problem with that. I was going to go there myself. You have my full cooperation from this point on. I don't want to get killed any more than you do, and me being treated like a prisoner means I can't defend myself against any Syrian lunatic that might intercept us. And trust me when I say, I have no qualms about killing Syrian soldiers or any of the types we're likely to encounter there. I just need to know one thing."

"And that is?"

131

"When will you be satisfied?"

"When we know the truth."

"Even if the truth is what's on that tablet?"

"That would be impossible. We are going there to prove it is blasphemous."

Acton leaned back, holding up both hands. "Fine, fine. I will get you there, I will tell you my opinion, then you will decide what to do with the information, correct?"

"Yes."

"Good. So, the moment I bring you to the location, then I give you my assessment, I'm free to go?"

"Yes."

His heart hammered. "And my wife? No harm will come to her?"

"None."

Acton smiled broadly and picked up his coffee. "Then, gentlemen, we have a deal. I'm part of the team."

The leader smirked. "Very well, Professor, but if at any time I sense otherwise, I'll make sure you see your wife die."

Operations Center 3, CIA Headquarters

Langley, Virginia

"Can we get any other footage from the area? We need to know if they're still inside, or if they left out the back or some other side entrance."

Child and the others worked the tapped video sources as Tong connected her headset. She dialed Leather's number as one of the images on the large display showed satellite footage of his team's vehicle as it turned onto the street where Acton had last been spotted.

"Hello?"

"It's me. It should be directly ahead. On your right, twenty meters."

"You're sure he's still inside?"

She glanced at the others, everyone either shrugging or throwing up their hands. "Negative. We have footage of him entering, but there could be other ways out that aren't covered."

"Understood." There was a pause. "Stand by." The voice changed, as if he were no longer talking to her. "They look like our guys, don't they?"

She snapped her fingers and Child zoomed in on the front of the café where two men had just stepped out wearing the same clothes from earlier.

"Affirmative. It looks like they might be getting ready to leave," said another voice in the background.

An SUV pulled up and the two men opened the doors on the passenger side. Three more stepped out from the café.

"That's Acton!" exclaimed Child, stating the obvious.

"I've got eyes on the target. Moving to intercept," said Leather.

"Understood," replied Tong as they watched Leather's SUV pass their target's then cut to the right, blocking them. Acton was shoved into the back as the others jumped inside, the doors slamming shut as the hostile driver put the vehicle in reverse and backed up before jerking the wheel to the left then quickly surged forward again, passing Leather's team as the man rushed toward his client.

A client leaning out the window with a gun, firing it at those seeking to save him.

Everyone sat stunned for a moment before Child finally broke the silence. "What the hell just happened?"

Tong sprang into action. "Follow that SUV. We need to know where they're taking him."

"Wherever the hell he wants, by the looks of it. He's working with them!"

"We don't know that. Now follow him." She activated her mic. "Ground team, report!"

Leather and the others checked on each other before he responded. "We're all right. No casualties. It looks like he wasn't aiming at us."

Her eyes narrowed. "Then who the hell was he aiming at?"

"Our tires. He took out two of our tires."

"We've got locals coming into the area!" announced Marc Therrien, one of the senior analysts, from the back of the room.

She gave him a thumbs-up. "Colonel, we've got locals inbound. Suggest you get out of there ASAP."

"Understood. Ground team, out."

The SUV was cleared of anything identifiable, then she monitored as the team split up, everyone blending into the crowd, each slowly changing their appearance as they did so.

These were pros, even if they didn't technically work for the CIA.

But they were not her primary concern. The question was why had Acton fired at those who could save him? Yet that's not what had happened. He had taken out their tires.

"He doesn't want them following him."

Child spun in his chair. "Huh?"

"He took out their tires. If he wanted them dead, he could have easily shot them. He's an expert shot. But instead, he took out their tires so they couldn't follow. He's still being coerced, but he's convinced them that he's on their side."

"How the hell did he manage that?"

"Because it's probably true," said Therrien. "This guy is an archaeology geek. He wants to know the truth as much as they do."

Tong disagreed. "He'd hardly put people's lives in danger just for that." She pursed her lips as she stared at a replay of the confrontation. "He's still being coerced. If he's rescued, then he can't fulfill his mission, which means they follow through on whatever threat they made."

"What's his mission?"

"Guiding them to the location indicated on the tablet would be my guess. He gets them there, and they let him go, cleaning the slate. He doesn't, they follow through."

"Killing his wife?" suggested Child.

"That would be my guess. Whatever it is, it's bad enough that he'd rather not only stay with them but warn us off as well."

"Then what are we supposed to do if he doesn't want our help?"

"Oh, he'll want our help, that I can guarantee you."

"What makes you say that?"

"Because he's heading into Syria, and there's no way in hell that's going to go well."

Istanbul, Turkey

"I told you they were good."

The leader frowned at Acton then flipped his fingers at him. "Gun."

Acton cleared it then handed it over, having liberated it from one of his captors only moments before. He had decided on the brash action for two reasons—one, he'd rather be the one shooting at Leather's team, and two, he had to send a message by shooting out their tires.

Back off.

"The next time you take one of our weapons, you're dead, and so is your wife."

Acton stared at the man. "Listen, I just did you a favor. They can't follow us now, and they're all alive. If one of you had fired, you would have killed innocent people. This way, we're all still relatively clean in all this. Nobody is dead, nobody is hurt, and all we've really done is stolen a tablet that in the end, we can return."

"The tablet will never be returned."

Acton seized the opportunity to dig a little deeper. "What do you mean?"

"If it is of historical significance, it will be placed in the Vault of Secrets. If it is fake, then it will be destroyed as the blasphemous forgery it is."

"If it's real, why wouldn't you destroy it?"

"Because we may be mistaken. Simply because you say it's real, doesn't necessarily mean you're correct. By preserving it, someday the truth might be revealed, then it can be safely destroyed. But until we know for certain, it shall be preserved."

Acton sighed. "I don't understand you people. You claim to want to protect the Church from any harm, yet you won't destroy something that could damage the Christian faith irrevocably. And how do you plan to get it in the Vault? Your way in was blocked."

"We don't need to get it inside the Vault. His Holiness will do that for us."

Acton's eyebrows shot up. "He will? That's mighty nice of him."

The man chuckled. "The tablet will be delivered to him, and he'll know what to do."

"You've done this before?"

"On many occasions. It is part of our mandate. The Vault is filled with things we've discovered, and that the clergy and others have discovered on their own over the millennia."

Acton leaned forward, a question begging to be asked. "And if we find what the tablet claims? What will you do then?"

The man bristled. "That, Professor Acton, will never happen."

Great Palace of Constantinople

Constantinople, Eastern Roman Empire

AD 1070

"Your husband does not fare well."

Eudokia regarded her brother-in-law, a most distasteful man, and thankfully not from her bloodline but that of her late husband. John Doukas, named Caesar as her husband died, was to have been co-regent with Michael Psellos until her son, also named Michael, was ready. But those were her husband's plans, not hers. She had quickly moved to sideline the two co-regents, instead ruling in the name of her sons as co-emperors, their mother pulling the strings of an empire.

It had infuriated the Doukai family of her late husband, and with Romanus now emperor for over two full years, with one son now blessing the marriage, and another child on the way, things were even worse. The Doukai were terrified of losing their brief claim to the throne, and she had to find a way to placate them until he returned, lest they take action and depose him while he fought for the empire.

139

"There have been some delays in his plans, mostly because of traitors that he already said were within our midst. It merely proves he was right, and once his reforms of the army are complete, we shouldn't face such things in the future."

"Ridding the empire of its dependence on mercenaries is no easy task."

"If it were easy, then it wouldn't take a great man to accomplish."

"A great man. You think highly of your husband, don't you?"

"Of course. He is my husband, the father of my youngest son, and my emperor."

"Yet I thought you married him for the good of the empire, not the good of your womanly desires."

She eyed the pig. She could order his throat slit this instant. It would take a single call to her guard who stood outside the door, then a flick of her wrist. It would be within her right, yet it would cause too many problems that could lead to the very rebellion she was attempting to avoid. "My womanly desires aside, I did what was best for the empire. We needed a strong leader with a military background who could take command of our armies and bring in the reforms necessary to restore the empire to its former glory."

"Former glory? I thought we were doing quite well before he came along."

"Then you are naïve, which is why I decided you were unfit to be co-regent."

John bristled, shifting in his chair. "If you weren't who you are, you would be whipped for your insolence."

Eudokia smirked at him. "And if you weren't who you are, I would have your throat slit for yours." She smiled. "Now that we have the pleasantries out of the way, I want you to hear my plan, so I may assuage you of any concerns you might have about the current situation."

John stared at her. "Your plan? What plan?"

"The plan I have had since the very moment I decided to marry Romanus. The plan I have kept to myself, and now share with you, since you have so brazenly attempted to turn my own son against me."

"I don't know of what you speak."

"Then what I have been told must be untrue, which is a relief. For if I had found proof, only your head would be appearing before me today."

John paled slightly, confirming everything she needed to know.

"Now, to my plan. Michael is to be emperor. Let there be no doubt of that. The Doukai bloodline will rule after Romanus, and his future sons will follow him."

John recovered his composure. "Does Romanus know this?"

"Yes. He understands that *I* rule behind the scenes. He is merely a figurehead, necessary to gain the respect of the army he is reforming. He will die in battle eventually, and when he does, Michael will assume the throne. Any child I bear with Romanus will be at least twenty years his junior. There is absolutely no threat to the Doukai claim to the throne."

"And should Romanus not die in battle?"

"Then glory be to the Roman Empire! If he does not die, and claims victory after victory, the power of the empire simply continues to grow, its future secured by his successes, and when he dies an old man, Michael will inherit a throne far more powerful than he would have."

141

"Old age? By then his sons will be old enough to challenge, and Michael could be an old man as well. And *you* could be dead."

She chuckled. "And you will likely be dead as well." She sighed, holding up her hands slightly. "Very well, I'll make you a promise, between you, me, and God. Should Romanus survive, on the tenth anniversary of his ascension, I will name Michael emperor, and Romanus will retire."

"Fantasy!"

She eyed him. "Excuse me?"

"No man will give up the throne of the greatest empire that has ever existed, on the say-so of a woman."

"You underestimate me, and you misunderstand him."

John laughed. "Oh, do please enlighten me!"

"Romanus doesn't desire power. He sought it to save the empire through rebuilding the army. He will step aside eagerly if he is allowed to maintain command, guided, of course, by Michael."

John shook his head. "Fine. I'll humor you. Let's say this is even plausible, what will you do if he decides to defy you?"

She leaned forward, all pleasantness gone. "Then I will slit his throat myself while he makes love to me." She jabbed a finger at John's shocked face. "There is nothing I won't do for my children, or my empire."

Istanbul Ataturk Airport

Istanbul, Turkey

Present Day

Laura rushed off her plane and into the charter terminal. Inside, she spotted Leather and his team waiting past customs. She was dying to speak to him. She had made certain before she left that she had full communications capabilities, unwilling to be out of touch as her husband had been. She had read all the updates and spoken to Reading and Leather on several occasions until things got violent.

Then Leather had issued the order.

No more open communications.

She still had the encrypted emails, so knew what had happened, but she wanted to speak to Leather directly, to hear what she couldn't believe. Her husband had opened fire on his own security team. Yes, that wasn't exactly what had happened according to the report, but it was how her mind was interpreting it.

She wanted more. She needed more. She needed to look into Leather's eyes and hear the words spoken. He had seen James' face as he fired. What was his expression? How had his eyes appeared? Was he frightened or angry? She had a million questions, yet had to control herself for the moment, as not only was she dealing with an on-edge customs official, several police were standing with Leather who no doubt wanted to question her about her husband.

She might not get that opportunity to speak to her head of security.

She cleared and rushed toward Leather, giving him a hug, the man returning it awkwardly. "I'm so glad you're here."

"Ma'am, this is Captain Demirel. He's with the Turkish Police Service. He has some questions for you."

"Professor Palmer, it's a pleasure. I wish it were under better circumstances."

She shook the man's hand. "As do I. How can I help you, Captain?"

"I need you to come to the station with me. I have some questions."

She tensed. "Am I under arrest?"

"No, of course not. This is simply routine."

"Then I'd prefer not to. How about we meet at my hotel in one hour, and I'll happily answer any questions you may have?"

The man wasn't pleased, but from his demeanor, she guessed Leather had informed him of how much money she and James had, and how well connected they were. "Very well. In one hour."

"Thank you." She turned to Leather. "Let's go."

He led her outside with nothing else said, and within minutes they were on the way to the hotel.

"They're following us," said a man from the driver's seat she didn't recognize, his accent suggesting a local hire.

"That's to be expected," replied Leather. "Just follow the rules of the road. Don't give them any reason to pull us over."

"Roger that."

"Professor Palmer, this is Vasif Irmak. He's a local contact who has been helping us."

"A pleasure, ma'am," said Irmak, peering at her through the rearview mirror.

"Likewise." She swiveled in her seat, facing Leather directly. "Tell me everything."

"You've read the reports?"

"Reports are facts. I need to get your sense of things. What's going on?"

"I think he was picked up here by the Keepers, taken to a secret location, a deal was struck—"

"What kind of deal?"

"Likely something along the lines of, I'll cooperate as long as you don't hurt my wife."

Her chest ached at the words. "Go on."

"They brought him to the dig site, he rendered Professor Boran unconscious—"

"Why do you think he did that? It's not like him to hurt someone who's innocent."

"He probably decided he couldn't take the risk the professor wouldn't cooperate. One shout and the new security would have been all over him and he would never have been able to steal the tablet. If the bargain was for your life, then he would never take that risk. He used his training to safely take out his opponent in a non-lethal manner, then used those purchased minutes to make his escape."

"The guards shot at him?"

"Yes, but you can hardly blame them. He was, after all, doing the very thing they were there to prevent."

She frowned. "I suppose, but next time let's make sure they have photos of us. If we're paying them, they shouldn't be trying to kill us."

"I'll make sure."

She leaned closer. "Now tell me, at the café, what did you see?"

"Two men—"

"No, his eyes. His face. When you saw him, what did you see?"

"When he came out of the café he seemed calm. He walked out freely and didn't appear to be looking for a means of escape."

"And when you intercepted them?"

"He leaned out the window, looked directly at me, and fired a handgun twelve times, taking out the two passenger-side tires of our vehicle, without wounding anyone, or missing a single shot, from all outward appearances."

"But his expression."

"Determined. And he made direct eye contact with me. In retrospect, it was as if he wanted me to know he knew who he was shooting at."

"And your interpretation?"

"He wants us to back off and let him do what needs to be done."

She sighed. "Which is go to the location on the tablet."

"That's the going theory. I think he's made a deal to help them get there, examine whatever is found, if anything, then they'll let him go and whatever threat they made will be rescinded. Ma'am, if they've threatened your life, he will do whatever it takes to make certain he accomplishes whatever it is they're demanding of him."

"Evidently so." She straightened in her seat and leaned her head back, closing her eyes. "What does Langley have to say?"

"Very little. They're acknowledging our reports but providing little data. Almost everything they're doing is classified and can't be shared with us civilians. All I can say is, I'm sure they're doing whatever they can to find him, but…"

She opened her eyes. "But?"

"Well, ma'am, if he goes into Syria, their hands might be tied."

She frowned. "Then we'll have to go in."

Leather's eyes shot wide. "Ma'am?"

"We go in after him."

"Ma'am, that's…unwise. It's a warzone. There are so many factions fighting there that no one is your friend."

"If the CIA isn't sending someone, then I'm going. Start making the arrangements."

"Ma'am, I hate to say this but you going is insane, and I can't be party to it. I suggest instead you start using your contacts to apply pressure for the American government to send in assets to rescue one of their citizens who has been kidnapped."

147

She glared at him for a moment then relented. He was right. She wanted to go save James, but she would likely get herself or those with her captured, wounded, or killed. This had to be left to the pros.

It was time to call in favors.

1st Special Forces Operational Detachment—Delta HQ

Fort Bragg, North Carolina

A.k.a. "The Unit"

Colonel Thomas Clancy sat behind his desk, wiggling his ass as he struggled to crack an uncrackable back, his sciatica driving him nuts. His doctor had told him to do some cobra yoga position thing, which sounded an awful lot like what he thought a downward dog was. He had never done yoga, and had no intention of starting now, but he was getting old and shit was falling apart.

A few of the guys had been shooting the shit at the mess last night, joking that they were considering retiring then heading to Ukraine to finally kill some Russians, since they'd been cheated out of that opportunity with the end of the Cold War. It was just old soldiers talking big after a few brews, but man, right now, the idea sounded fantastic.

If it weren't for their nukes, we could go in right now and take them out.

The Russian Army had proven incompetent, poorly equipped and supplied, with troops unwilling and unable to fight. They had shown that

149

Russia was no longer a real threat to anyone, their only genuinely terrifying weapon their nuclear arsenal. Yet even that, if it were maintained as well as the rest of their forces, might not be the threat the West thought it was, not to mention the fact there was no proverbial button. The maniac in charge couldn't just press a button and launch. All he could do was order the launch, then hopefully someone in the chain of command would shoot the piece of shit in the head and save the world a lot of headaches.

Someone had to kill him, but it had to be a Russian, otherwise the country might galvanize behind their dead nutbar and cause a real problem.

The incompetence on the battlefield explained why the Russians were using Wagner Group so frequently. Wagner was a private gun-for-hire outfit, primarily ex-Russian military, heavily concentrated on the Spetsnaz side of things. They had been used extensively in Syria and Libya, and were now rumored to be heading into Ukraine. They were effective and brutal, as they didn't follow the same rules as soldiers, and they all wanted to be there—the money was exceptional.

It reminded him of the mercenaries of old, when the great empires of history began farming out their wars, even their own security, to those other than their own citizens, who preferred to enjoy the spoils of what had been gained by past generations. It was always a sign of decline when a country didn't believe enough in what it was doing to hire out the dirty work rather than do it themselves.

Like today with Russia, or his own country in Iraq and Afghanistan, or so many other shitholes around the world where America wanted a presence but too often sent in private contractors.

Maybe it's time to retire.

He could. He had enough years in, his wife was itching to spend more time with him, and he wasn't happy with where the world was heading. Maybe now was the time to get out, collect his pension, and leave the future to the younger generation.

Yet he loved his job and loved the men and women under his command even more. He couldn't leave them to what was coming up the chain behind him. They didn't have the experience, and too many of them embraced ideals he simply couldn't understand or support.

Though perhaps there was hope. Russia had assumed NATO was weak, that the West was weak. It had assumed it could simply take Ukraine, and nothing would be done to stop them. They were wrong and had paid a heavy price. Perhaps this was the wake-up call the world needed. The naïve notion that everyone just wanted to live in peace and harmony was bullshit. Everyone who served overseas knew that. But too many in the halls of power, or the experts on Hollywood Squares, thought everything could be negotiated, all that was needed was trade agreements and hugs. Those were all good, as long as they were backed by a military willing and able to act should things go wrong.

He sighed.

I guess I better stick around a while longer.

His phone rang, which startled him. It never rang. All his calls routed through his assistant sitting in the outer office. He picked up the handset. "Hello?"

"Colonel Clancy?"

"Yes? Who is this? How did you get this number?"

"I'm patching Professor Palmer in now."

His eyebrows shot up. Laura Palmer and her husband were two royal pains in his ass, but also the best damned civilians he had ever encountered. They had helped save his men on numerous occasions, and had done some truly unselfish things, like setting up a college fund for Spock's daughter when Joanne had been killed recently.

Not to mention funding the revenge mission to Moscow.

He always had time for them, though he never wanted to talk to them.

"Hello, Colonel, are you there?"

"Hello, Professor. Ahh, how did you get this number? Even I don't know it."

She laughed. "Even I know not to ask that question, sir. My travel agent is exceptional."

"She must be. I assume there is something important going on, and it has to do with your husband since I'm speaking to you."

"Yes, sir. James has been kidnapped by a group called the Keepers of the One Truth. Bravo Team encountered them a few years ago."

Clancy recalled the mission. "Yes, I'm aware of who they are. You say Professor Acton has been kidnapped by them. Where and when?" He leaned forward and began taking notes.

"Earlier today in Istanbul. I'm going to have a secure email sent to you with all the details. Here's the urgent thing. We believe they're taking him to Syria in an attempt to find the burial site of Jesus Christ. My security chief, Cameron Leather, tells me it is a highly volatile region and James is in serious danger."

Clancy's eyes narrowed. "Wait a minute. Did you say the burial site of Jesus Christ? Isn't that in Jerusalem? Church of the Holy Sepulcher or something like that?"

"Let's just say that a discovery has been made that suggests otherwise."

Clancy slumped back in his chair. What kind of horseshit was the woman talking about? "This is a joke, right?"

"I'm afraid not, Colonel. I'm not saying it's true, all I'm saying is that we found evidence, a tablet, that suggests it might be. The Keepers are zealots, so they're determined to keep the truth, whatever that may be, from the world, and they're using James to do it."

Clancy shook his head. This took the cake, then again, Dawson and the others swore they had seen the Ark of the Covenant with these two, so anything was possible. The fact it could be true was disturbing, however. He was a good Christian, though rarely attended church. He worshipped in the privacy of his own home, and in his own way. To think, however, that what he believed to be true with Jesus Christ might not be, shook him more than he would have thought.

But she was right. It didn't matter if it were true or not, all that mattered was that an American citizen, and a good friend to the Unit, had been kidnapped, and was either now in, or soon would be in, enemy territory.

"What are you asking of me?"

"Can you send a team in to get him?"

"Syria is a big country, Professor. We can't just waltz in and start asking around."

"Colonel, I can give you the exact coordinates of where he'll be. You just need to wait for him to arrive, then send in an extraction team."

Clancy smiled slightly. This might just be doable, with little collateral damage. Then again, this was Professor Acton, and things never went smoothly when he was involved.

"I'll get back to you shortly."

Operations Center 3, CIA Headquarters
Langley, Virginia

Two extra-strength Tylenol, a fistful of milk thistle, and three bottles of water along with a long, hot shower and plenty of coffee had Leroux feeling almost human.

Almost.

Sherrie, who could hold her liquor far better than him, had thankfully driven him in—he was in no condition to be on the roads. In fact, he might legally not be in any condition to run an op. But this wasn't an ordinary op. There were no assets being deployed, no agents on the ground. They were in observer mode where he couldn't do much damage even if he tried.

He cleared the ops center security then entered the room, squinting at the intense light from the displays to his left. His team hailed him in an exaggeratedly loud manner, no doubt punishing him for having called them in unexpectedly, then not bothering to show up himself.

He batted a hand at them as he nodded. "Yeah, yeah, I deserved that, but if you were as drunk as I was, you would never have come in either. I'm sure there's some regulation that says you can't be in an ops center legally hammered."

Child eyeballed him. "You sure you're sober?"

Leroux pointed at Child's face. "You've got half a bag of Cheetos on your face. You savin' those for later?"

The room roared and Child spun in his chair, giving them a collective middle finger before furiously brushing at his face.

"Clean up on aisle four!" shouted Therrien, eliciting another round of laughter and another one-finger salute.

Leroux dropped his bag at his station then faced the room. "I'm sorry I'm late, everyone. I blame Dylan, and for those of you who know him, you'll believe me. And by the way, beer and amaretto really do taste like Dr. Pepper, which makes it a deadly combo when that's your favorite soda."

Therrien laughed. "At least you weren't taken out by Alabama Slammers, or Alalama Lammas as I call them at two in the morning. Those things will kick the shit out of you the next day."

"I'll keep that in mind." Leroux dropped into his chair, his entire body protesting at the stupidity of being here. He was confident he was legal, though his mind was a fog that had barely begun to clear. The coffee he was filled with, something he hated, wasn't helping his protesting stomach. He pulled out a breakfast burrito, the last part of his breakfast of champions Sherrie had picked him up along the way, and

156

unwrapped it. It promptly fell apart, the wrap a complete mess and an insult to burritos the world over.

He cursed.

"What's wrong?" asked Tong, turning in her chair.

He wrapped the mess back up, noticing how cold it was, and tossed it into the garbage bin by his desk. "Disappointing burrito."

"McDogFood?" asked Child.

"Yup."

"Never get the burrito. Better than fifty-fifty you'll be disappointed."

"I took a gamble and lost." Leroux sighed. "Okay, bring me up to date."

Tong fed him the latest goings-on. He had read the updates on the way in, so there was little new except that they had lost Acton's vehicle in a camera dead zone that Tong was convinced the Keepers were aware of. A switch was probably made, and there had been no sightings since.

Laura was on the ground, safe with Leather, but was currently being interrogated by the Turkish authorities at her hotel. That was a concern. If they took a genuine interest in her, or thought she was involved in any way, they could hold her indefinitely, and there would be little anyone could do unless her connections were willing to raise a diplomatic stink.

This situation was getting out of hand. The moment Acton had been kidnapped, Laura should have been locked in a room so she couldn't rush off to join in the search. It should have been left to professionals like Leather and his local contacts, and the local authorities should have been brought in right away. Instead, because of the Keepers' involvement, it had taken on a mysterious air that was complicating things.

The door to the operations center hissed open and their boss, Leif Morrison entered. He glanced at the screens, which showed little, then eyeballed Leroux, a smile spreading.

"You look like shit."

Leroux grunted as he struggled to his feet. "I feel like shit."

"Have you found him yet?"

"Negative. We're confident he's being taken to Syria."

"Yes, so I've gathered."

Leroux's eyes narrowed. "Sir?"

Morrison dropped into a spare chair and Leroux thankfully returned to his own, his knees shaking slightly. "You'll never believe who Palmer just called."

"Who?"

"Colonel Clancy."

Leroux glanced at Tong, equally surprised. "How? I mean, it's not like he takes calls."

"Clancy just called me. He said she somehow called his desk directly. Bypassed the switchboard and his assistant."

Leroux chuckled. "Sometimes I think they're better connected than we are. He couldn't have been impressed."

"Well, like he said to me, he has a lot of time for them. They financed that little Moscow thing and set up a college fund for Spock's kid. There's not a man on that team that wouldn't lay down their lives for them."

"And they'd do the same," said Tong.

Morrison turned in his chair and nodded. "Well said." He returned his attention to Leroux. "So, new plan. We know where they're taking Acton. We're sending Bravo Team in to retrieve him as soon as you spot him. She's going to be sending coordinates soon so we can start monitoring and pre-positioning assets. As soon as you have the coordinates, start monitoring the area. I want to know just what our guys are getting into."

"Yes, sir."

Morrison rose and headed for the door. "Oh, and Chris?"

"Yes, sir?"

"You still smell like a brewery. Go have a shit, shower, and shave then a nap. I don't want you passing out when we're in the middle of the op."

Leroux flushed as everyone snickered. "Yes, sir."

The door shut and he turned to Tong. "Am I really that bad?"

She lowered her voice. "I'd never say anything—"

"But I will," interrupted Child. "Dude, you smell like a dive bar on a Saturday morning."

Laughter erupted and it was Leroux's turn to spin in his chair, a middle finger extended high over his head.

Park Hyatt Istanbul Macka Palas

Istanbul, Turkey

Laura had told Captain Demirel everything except for one crucial detail—the fact she knew who her husband's abductors were. Mentioning the Keepers of the One Truth would simply complicate things. Demirel might believe her and treat them as the threat they were, which could put James in danger, or he might not, and think it so absurd, he'd assume she was attempting to hide something, so arrest her for being involved.

"Do you have anything else to add?"

She shook her head. "No, though I do have a question."

"Of course."

"I realize nothing I can say can convince you that my husband is absolutely innocent here, but can I at least assume you will give him the benefit of the doubt and not shoot him when you try to arrest him?"

Demirel regarded her for a moment. "That all depends on your husband."

160

She tensed. "What do you mean?"

"If he fires at us as he fired at his own security team, then we will have no choice but to defend ourselves."

She frowned. "As I explained, he was warning them off. He shot out the tires so they couldn't pursue them."

"Yes, an academic, an archaeology professor of all things, fired twelve perfect shots from a moving vehicle."

Leather cleared his throat. "All twelve were hits?"

Demirel nodded. "An impressive feat."

Leather, the proud teacher, exchanged a grin with one of his men. "I'll say."

"You are apparently a very good teacher, but I'll ask you this. Where did he get the gun? Even if he is cooperating to protect someone, perhaps his wife here, they would never give him a gun."

"They must have," said Laura, sensing where this was going.

"Or he took it off one of them," suggested Leather.

Demirel rose. "Either they gave him the gun, which means he's working with them and they trust him implicitly, which means he wasn't abducted at all but was merely met by his partners in this crime, or he took it off them, and is most likely dead for doing so." He headed for the door as Laura rose.

"What now?"

"I would prefer it if you would remain in the city, however, I have no reason to hold you. Even if you are involved, I already have Interpol asking questions, and the last thing I need is more paperwork if I bring you in. You are free to enjoy our city or leave the country." He paused with his hand on the doorknob. "I will suggest only one thing, Professor."

"What's that?"

"Don't go to Syria."

Great Palace of Constantinople

Constantinople, Eastern Roman Empire

AD 1071

"Things are not going well on the battlefield, my love."

Romanus regarded his wife as she lay in the bed, naked, her thighs half covered by a sheet, the rest of her skin bare and glistening from their vigorous activities ended only moments before. He stood nearby, quenching his thirst, but paused at her words. "What do you mean?"

"My advisors tell me we have suffered many defeats over the past year. They question why you continue to press to the south when we aren't ready."

He frowned at her then resumed his refreshment, using it as a delay to answer her. He had never told her of the tablet. He had never wanted her faith shaken as his had been. He loved her too much for that. Yet a wife shouldn't question a husband, not when it came to affairs beyond her.

"Who has been telling you such nonsense?"

"You know very well that I have my own trusted advisors, who are well aware of all that goes on within the empire."

"They shouldn't be troubling you with such things."

She sat up, covering herself with the sheet, signaling an end to any further activities should this conversation go poorly. "I am empress. My sons are co-emperors. It is my duty to know what goes on in my empire. And remember our agreement."

He played with her a little bit. "Our agreement?"

"You rule in name only. *I* and my son Michael are the true rulers of the Roman Empire."

"Many would question that, since I sit on the throne and wear the crown."

She glared at him. "Are you reneging on our agreement?"

He chuckled. "And if I did?"

She rose, the sheet and her nakedness forgotten to her, her full rage directed at him. "Then I would have you killed."

He paused, ogling her incredible body as he took another drink. "I think you would."

"I would do anything to protect my children, and my empire."

He put down his cup and strode toward the bed, his own nakedness not forgotten on him. His hand darted out and he grabbed her by the chin, gripping her hard. "You dare threaten your emperor?"

She kicked him in the balls and he doubled over in agony, his grip broken as she withdrew, opening a nearby drawer and drawing a dagger. "You dare assault me? I put you where you are today! And I keep you there! If it weren't for me, you'd be long dead, murdered by the Doukai family."

He sat on the edge of the bed, cupping his balls, wincing. "What are you talking about?"

"They believe you scheme to keep the throne for your family. I have been assuring them that we have an agreement that Michael will assume the throne when you are done rebuilding the empire. But now I see that they were right. That you do intend to keep the throne."

He eyed the dagger. "And what do you plan on doing with that?"

"I intend to cut your balls off."

He laughed then crossed his legs, wincing again at the move. "My love, I have no intention of keeping the throne. It is yours. It always has been. I am grateful to you for sparing my life, and we made an agreement before God. I intend to keep it, and hopefully my balls, should you allow it."

She relaxed slightly, though didn't lower the dagger. "Then what was all that nonsense about?"

"I had intended to have a little fun with you, then you angered me, and I overreacted. I'm under a tremendous amount of stress. There's more going on than I've told you."

She lowered the dagger. "Of what do you speak?"

"You don't want to know."

"I'm your wife and empress. I deserve to know, and I must know."

He sighed, uncrossing his legs and groaning. "If I tell you, there is no un-telling you. You can never unknow what I know, and believe me when I tell you, you will wish you could."

She approached and he turned his legs away from her, protecting his nether region. She smiled apologetically. "Don't worry, I'm not going to hurt you. Touch me like that again, and I will cut them off, however."

He eyed the dagger. "I'd believe you more if you put that away."

She giggled and returned the blade to the drawer from which it came then sat beside him. He spread his legs and moved to hold his scrotum when she reached out and cupped him, her cool hands causing him to sigh. "Does that feel better?"

"You have no idea."

"Now, tell me what I want to know, before I squeeze them off." She smiled mischievously, though he couldn't be entirely certain whether she was joking.

"We found something in Hierapolis."

Her eyebrows rose slightly. "What?"

"A tablet. Written in Hebrew with a translation and a note from Rashid al-Dawla Mahmud."

"The Emir of Aleppo?"

"I see you are well-informed."

"Continue. What did this tablet say?"

He hesitated. "Are you sure you want to know? It will change everything you believe forever."

She regarded him. "Has it changed your beliefs?"

He sighed. "I...I'm not sure. It has certainly shaken my faith. It has me questioning everything."

Her eyes narrowed. "Your faith? You mean your faith in God?"

His shoulders slumped. "Not in God, I suppose, but in Jesus Christ."

166

She gasped and involuntarily squeezed. He groaned in agony and she let go immediately. "Sorry." She curled her leg up under her, facing him. "What do you mean you're questioning your faith in Jesus Christ?"

He leaned closer, lowering his voice. "I mean, if the tablet is genuine, and the bishop killed himself believing it was—"

"You mean he committed suicide because of what you found?"

"Yes."

"I thought they had claimed temporary demonic possession."

"That was the cover story. Only Alexander and I know of the tablet."

Her eyebrows rose. "Nobody else has seen it?"

"Nobody else alive."

"You mean—"

"I had no choice, and you'll understand when I tell you what it said."

"Tell me!"

"It said that Jesus Christ was never resurrected from the dead. It said that His bones were taken away and hidden in a location indicated on the tablet, and the story of His resurrection was a lie by His disciples to continue His teachings."

She recoiled in horror at the very notion. "Certainly it can't be true!"

He shrugged. "I don't know, but I have been trying to prove it one way or the other."

"How?"

"By taking the territory where the tablet indicates his bones lie."

She gasped as her jaw dropped. "You mean all these battles, these premature pushes south, are all in an attempt to find the bones of Jesus Christ?"

"Yes."

Her eyes shot wide. "And if you find them—"

"It means that he was never resurrected as we've been taught, but instead, his body was taken from his tomb and hidden somewhere else."

"Who would do such a thing?"

"I don't know. It could have been one or more of the disciples, so they could concoct a story where the tomb was found empty, and the discovery would lend credence to the resurrection lie. Or perhaps someone who didn't want to risk that it was true, so they took the body and hid it somewhere."

She thought for a moment then shook her head. "That would make no sense. If He were resurrected, then it wouldn't matter where his body was. He would simply come back to life and visit His disciples."

Romanus chewed his cheek, processing his wife's words. She was right, it did make no sense, and it left only one explanation. "The disciples must have done it. It must have been their plan all along."

She closed her eyes, tears escaping the corners. "So, what are we saying? Are we saying that Jesus Christ was just a man who spoke eloquently? Just a man who lived and died, and never was the Son of God any more than the rest of us?"

He slowly shook his head as he wrapped an arm around her shoulders. "I don't know. Now you can see why I have been so tortured. I don't know what the truth is, but I must find out. If I can take the territory referred to in the tablet, and find that there is no body there, then we can confirm it is a fake."

"And if you do find a body?"

"Then we will have to decide what to do next. Preserve the beliefs of our citizens, or reveal the truth, and perhaps destroy the empire in the process."

Unknown Location

Turkey

Present Day

Acton's ass was killing him. After he shot out the tires, they had driven for less than five minutes before switching vehicles. Half an hour later they were on the outskirts of Istanbul, then changed into a beat-up delivery van. Hours in the back of that with no air conditioning or shocks to speak of, and they were in yet another vehicle, this one making him miss the van.

Welcome to the backdoor into Syria while on the run from the law.

There had been little conversation from his side of things, and he was content to sit quietly and sip his water and eat the food provided him. His captors were much more relaxed around him now than earlier. It might be because he had fired on his own people, or that there was nothing he could do to them now that they were so far from civilization.

Or perhaps a bit of both.

But their relaxation had let certain things slip. They were all still speaking mostly Italian, but the language was similar enough to many others he was well aware of that he could pick up quite a few words.

Including names.

He had determined that the leader was Esposito, and the three others were Greco, Bianchi, and Russo. He had no idea who was in the front of the vehicle, as they changed each time they switched. It was clear the Keepers were well connected in Turkey, which made sense considering Constantinople was a major center of Christianity for a thousand years. There was a lot of history there related to the Church and the Christian faith.

It had given him time to think about what had happened in the past. Romanus had obviously discovered the tablet somehow. This Alexander person must have been entrusted with it, since the history of Romanus' betrayal and death was well documented. There was no way he could have hung on to a tablet under those circumstances. It meant someone else had it. He was buried where he died, which was the piece of history unknown until now, and was buried with the tablet, obviously with the blessing of the monks who had inhabited the island back then. It made him wonder if they were even aware of what was on the tablet, as it was unlikely they read Hebrew.

Alexander had left behind a tablet of his own, revealing the secret burial location, hinting at its own secret, likely fulfilling a promise made to Romanus before he died. It suggested that they were friends, perhaps best friends. His message to the future beseeched someone to discover the truth, and now that responsibility had fallen on him.

If it weren't for where they were heading, he might be able to focus more on what lay ahead. If the danger were eliminated, it was still a scary proposition he faced. If the tablet told the truth, that Jesus Christ hadn't been resurrected from the dead, and that instead his bones had been taken from his tomb and hidden away so that they could fake the discovery of his vacant burial site then claim his resurrection, it changed everything.

Everything.

And he wasn't certain he wanted that responsibility. What would his tombstone say? Here lies James Acton, destroyer of Christianity? And was it something he should reveal if it were true? Who was he to destroy someone's faith? Yes, he was a scientist. He should only be concerned with the facts, and if he discovered the bones of Jesus Christ, then that was a scientific fact, and it deserved to be made public so that it could be studied and debated.

He shook his head. His raging internal debate had neglected to take into account one important thing. Whose bones they might find. Just because they found bones didn't necessarily mean they belonged to Jesus. They could be anyone's bones. There was no possible way to know for certain. They would analyze the bones, determine when the man died, at what age, what his ancestry might be, was there anything to indicate the man had suffered some disease or injury inconsistent with what was known about Jesus and his upbringing.

There was a lot of science that would happen before anything could even be postulated. But with so little being known, since the Bible was written long after his death mostly by people who weren't there, all they could really rely on were the numbers. When they died, and how old were they when they died. Little more. And even if they could never say that it was indeed Jesus, the haters would be out in droves using just the suggestion of the possibility to tear down what had been built over two thousand years.

And again, he asked himself whether he wanted to be involved. Yes, his curiosity demanded to know the truth, but then there was also his responsibility to mankind. Yes, knowledge should be shared in principle, but that wasn't always true. This wasn't like hiding the cure for cancer, this would be hiding a possible truth that could bring nothing but harm.

He regarded his captors, a cheerful conversation taking place between them. If it weren't for the situation, and he were to see them at a café talking as they were now, he'd assume four close friends having a good time. Yet they had taken on the task of protecting the Church from anything that could bring it harm. Perhaps it was more than wanting their beliefs challenged. Perhaps they had known all along what he had just realized.

Sometimes the truth can be far more dangerous than the ignorance it threatened to replace.

The drone of the engine changed and they slowed. It had happened dozens of times during the hours spent in the back of the truck, but this time his companions were reacting.

"What's going on?" he asked.

"We're switching vehicles," said the leader, Esposito. "Just do as you're told and everything will be fine." He leaned closer. "And pull a stunt like you did before, and I'll shoot you myself."

Acton/Palmer Residence

St. Paul, Maryland

"Cameron is talking to some of his local contacts to see if he can get his team in. I'm—"

Reading frowned at the phone sitting on the table, everyone huddled around it. "You are *not* going to Syria."

Laura sighed. "No, I'm not. Cameron has convinced me that I'd just be a liability. A Western woman is too hard to explain there and I could jeopardize the mission. The important thing here is to get James to safety."

Reading leaned back, relieved. "Thank bloody hell for that. Do we know how much time we have?"

"Cameron says it would take a full day to drive there, but that doesn't take into account using backroads, or how they'll even get across the border. I doubt we'll see James at the final destination before end of day tomorrow."

"Please tell me you're going to leave Turkey and wait things out somewhere safer where you don't run the risk of arrest?"

"The gentleman I spoke to indicated I was free to leave. I don't think there's a risk of that anymore."

Reading's eyes rolled back. "You're a smart woman. He's baiting you. If you try to leave, it makes you look guilty. If you stay, then he can pick you up at any time. I just spoke to Michelle and her contacts are telling her they're still not sure about you, and the only reason they haven't arrested you is because of your money and connections. I say get the hell out of there now. If they let you leave, then great, and if they don't, then we'll know the truth."

"I'm not coming home. Not with James still out there."

"I'm not suggesting that. Let's get you somewhere safe."

"The choices are pretty slim in this region. If I want to get closer to the action, about the only safe place would be Israel."

Reading shook his head. "No, I had something else in mind. Why don't you go to Rome? Mario is there, and he can keep you completely wired in. From there you can be anywhere you need to be in the region within a couple of hours. You'll be safe there."

"That's a good idea. I'll have Mary make the arrangements and let Mario know I'm coming."

"I've already taken care of Mario. He's expecting you."

Laura chuckled. "Oh, I should have known I was being manipulated into your plan all along."

Reading laughed. "And you fell right into it. Now, call Mary, get your arse on that plane, and get to Rome as quickly as possible. The sooner you're all out of Turkey, the sooner I can get some sleep."

"Don't worry about me, Hugh, I'll be fine."

"Famous last words. Now go. We'll talk when you're on the plane."

"Talk to you soon."

Reading ended the call and turned to the others. "Well, that went better than I expected."

Mai agreed. "Probably because she knows Delta is going in to get him."

"Do you think they'll let her leave?" asked Tommy.

Reading sighed. "If I were in charge of the investigation, there's no way in hell."

Undisclosed Location

Syria

Sergeant Leon "Atlas" James held up a pair of tighty-whities hanging from the end of his M4. "Why are these hanging outside my window?"

Sergeant Carl "Niner" Sung glanced over his shoulder at his massively muscled friend, then returned his attention to the binoculars he was peering through, monitoring Wagner Group activity. "What makes you think they're mine?"

"You've labeled them."

"What? You mean I wrote my name in them? I'm sure I wouldn't be that stupid. What if I was captured? They give me one wedgie and they have my identity."

"Yeah, they'd be looking up who the hell Eugene Groebe is."

Sergeant Will "Spock" Lightman cocked an eyebrow. "Eugene Groebe? Where do I know that name from?"

Command Sergeant Major Burt "Big Dog" Dawson chuckled. It was a tradition at the Unit to get together once a month and have a classic eighties movie night. One senselessly violent movie followed by a ridiculous comedy. It was an era where movies were movies. No political correctness run amok, just good ole entertainment. It was a great way to relieve stress and build camaraderie among this team of America's elite. They were 1st Special Forces Operational Detachment—Delta, known to the public as the Delta Force, and each unit was a tight-knit group of men who would die for each other and their country without hesitation.

They were family.

They were brothers.

"Joysticks," said Niner.

A round of "oh yeahs" circled their accommodations. Today they were in Syria, inserted a few days ago to monitor Wagner Group activity. Wagner were mostly Russian mercenaries, brutal bastards who had no morals. They had been used effectively in several regional conflicts, and there was concern they might be moved into Ukraine to cause havoc there with no Geneva Convention concerns. His team, along with several others, had been sent into Syria to monitor them for any signs they were being redeployed, and to pick up any chatter that might be floating about.

"Jimmy, wasn't it your dad that recommended that one?" asked Atlas behind him.

Sergeant Gerry "Jimmy Olsen" Hudson replied. "Yup. You know, he said when he first saw that as a teenager, he thought the graphics in the video game were incredible."

"He was a gamer?"

"He went to arcades. Apparently, 1943 was his game."

Niner cooed. "I've played that on an emulator. Fun. That movie? Not so much."

Atlas' deep voice rumbled across the room as he tossed the underwear at Niner. "Then it's agreed. Jimmy's dad can't recommend movies anymore." He settled into position. "That still doesn't explain why you labeled your underwear."

"I didn't want to get them mixed up with yours."

Snickers filled the room.

"What?"

Jimmy laughed. "Dude, those tiny little things you wear wouldn't even get over the big man's foot."

Sergeant Eugene "Jagger" Thomas snorted. "If you wore Atlas', you could pull them up over your shoulders like Borat."

Atlas roared. "Now that I'd pay to see. I'll take them off right here, right now if you say you'll do it."

Niner gave him a look. "You just want to see me naked."

"You'll still have your shirt on, little man, and besides, there's nothing of yours I haven't seen before."

Niner grinned at him. "Ooh, I didn't think you were watching."

Spock sighed. "Dude, half the damn base has seen your dangler."

Jagger laughed. "Remember the time you two disappeared for two days and Spaz put up missing persons posters in the barracks for you?"

Niner groaned. "He didn't put up posters of us. He had side-by-side dick-pics."

Atlas chuckled. "I forgot about that. Man, Spaz was always doing crazy shit."

"I hate to speak ill of the dead, but the bastard put up a picture of a micro-penis with my name above it."

"You mean that wasn't you?"

Niner flipped him the bird over his shoulder as he continued peering through his binoculars. "What, and that other thing was supposed to be you?"

Atlas shrugged. "I thought it was a little small, to be honest."

Dawson rolled his eyes. "You do realize how much shit Spaz got into for that? He's just lucky I spotted the posters and got most of them down before the wrong person saw them. It's the modern army, gentlemen. You can't be putting shit like that up."

Niner stuck his tongue out at him. "You're no fun."

"I keep you guys employed by saving you from yourselves. Sometimes it's like babysitting teenagers on a school trip."

"And we thank you for it, BD," said Jimmy.

Atlas held up a finger. "Wait, where do we stand on Niner wearing my underwear?"

Dawson's earpiece squawked and he held up a fist, silencing the room.

"Zero-One, Control Actual. Come in, over."

Dawson's eyebrows rose. It was unusual for Colonel Clancy himself to come on the line. "This is Zero-One. Go ahead."

"We've got new orders for you, Zero-One. You're never going to guess who called the direct line to my desk earlier."

"Your sister-in-law?"

Snickers in the room and laughter on the other end of the line. "No, but good guess. Professor Palmer. Her husband has been kidnapped, and they believe he's being taken into Syria to find some ancient burial site. I've sent all the details as we know them to your secure messenger. Your team is being reassigned to Langley. They'll be Control for this op."

"Understood."

"Good luck, Zero-One. Go get our man. Control Actual, out."

Dawson smiled slightly. Clancy had referred to Acton as one of the team. In a way, the professors were. They were definitely family, and they had fought side-by-side on too many occasions to not count them as comrades in arms. He pulled out his tablet as his comms squawked again, this time replaced by Leroux's voice, a man he had worked with many times.

"Zero-One, Control Actual. Do you read, over?"

"Affirmative, Control."

"Good to be working with you again. Have you had a chance to review the intel package?"

Dawson opened the folder. "Negative. I've just brought it up. I assume you have our current location?"

"Affirmative. Your destination isn't too far from where you are. You have local transportation?"

"Yes, but travel isn't advisable unless absolutely necessary."

"We need you to get about seventy klicks to the southwest. That's where we believe Acton will be by end of day tomorrow."

Dawson's eyes narrowed. "Wait, how do you know where he's going to be tomorrow, but you don't know where he is today?"

"Read the package, Zero-One. It explains everything. You're going to love this one. Control, out."

Dawson brought up the summary written by one of Leroux's analysts, and his eyebrows shot up.

"What's going on, BD?" asked Atlas.

Dawson shook his head slowly. "You're not going to believe this shit, but apparently we might be about to meet Jesus Christ."

Great Palace of Constantinople

Constantinople, Eastern Roman Empire

AD 1071

"Your husband has failed."

Eudokia glared at Caesar John Doukas, accompanied by his coconspirator, Michael Psellos, the two men having barged into the throne room with dozens of their own guards. This was the situation she had struggled to avoid, yet the reports of the defeat in Manzikert were simply too much to overcome.

The coup was inevitable, and today, apparently, was to be its day.

The story spread by the traitorous Andronicus Doukas was that Romanus had faltered in battle, and the men had fled in the mistaken belief that their emperor was dead. The truth was far more sinister. Accounts of the fight from those loyal to her husband indicated that a flag on the battlefield had been misinterpreted by some as a signal that Romanus had fallen, and that Andronicus had capitalized on that, spreading the word among the soldiers that it was true, then ordered their retreat from the front.

With a significant portion of his forces gone, Romanus was left with diminished numbers to face the massive enemy force. He fought valiantly, though ultimately in vain. He had been captured and disgraced when the Seljuk Sultan Alp Arslan placed his foot on her husband's neck in ritual humiliation. He was then treated like a king, and a significant ransom was negotiated. Her husband had apparently been released and was on his way home, though without his armies, and without his honor.

He might yet survive this, if she managed the situation properly.

She rose. "He failed because Andronicus betrayed him."

"Nonsense. Your husband fell in battle and Andronicus ordered the retreat to preserve the army from slaughter."

"Yet my husband lives."

"We know that now."

She sneered. "Andronicus knew that then."

John grunted. "For enough gold, anyone will tell you what you want to hear. I choose to believe Andronicus, and regardless of what the truth is, your husband, our glorious emperor, was not only captured, but humiliated. And now we are forced to pay not only a large lumpsum ransom, but an annual payment as well."

"A pittance to secure the release of one's emperor."

"He's no longer my emperor."

"Nor mine," said Psellos.

She regarded the pathetic example of a man. "I couldn't care less what you think." She returned her attention to John, the greater threat in the room, as Psellos' cheeks flushed. "You dare challenge your emperor?"

"Like I said, he is no longer my emperor. My men are inside the palace, they hold all the key grounds, and most of our citizens believe Romanus is dead. It is time to settle this situation once and for all."

"And just how are we to settle this?"

"In a manner that I believe you will find quite satisfactory."

Her heart hammered, yet she kept her fear hidden. She could be about to die, and she intended to maintain her dignity. But more importantly, her children could be about to meet the sword. "Speak."

"Nobody will die here today, as long as you cooperate."

She relaxed slightly, though her heart still raced. "Continue."

"You will step down as empress and retire to a monastery. Your husband, when he returns, will do the same."

"You expect an emperor to retire to such a life?"

John smirked. "And your son, Michael, co-emperor with your husband, will, today, declare Romanus deposed. This will in effect make Michael emperor, your intention all along if you are to be believed, and Romanus merely a defeated general, returning home in humiliation. What better way to avoid such enduring humiliation by retiring out of the sight of the people he once ruled?"

She steadied her breathing as her mind raced. If John were to be trusted, which she doubted he could be, then no one would die, and in exile, Romanus could perhaps gather his supporters and retake the throne. Yet was that what she really wanted? Her intention all along was for Michael to be emperor, to lead the empire as he was destined to. For now, all she wanted was for Romanus to survive these events, and perhaps they could be reunited in time as husband and wife. With her son emperor, they could perhaps one day return to the palace, and if not, at least live a good, happy life, away from the trials and tribulations the halls of power brought.

"What say you?"

She frowned. "I agree." She raised a finger before John's smile could spread too far. "Provisionally."

Psellos growled. "What nonsense is this?"

She ignored the man, keeping her eyes on John. "Silence your dog lest I perceive him to be master here."

John's eyes flared and he whispered something to Psellos, who glared at him but took a step back nonetheless.

"Good. I will retire to a monastery of my choice, with a reasonable staff to see to my needs, and a stipend to allow me to live a lifestyle suitable to a woman of means. In exchange, I will withdraw completely from public life, and will only return to the palace should I be invited by the emperor. Agreed?"

John bowed slightly. "Agreed."

"I will instruct Michael to declare Romanus deposed, on the condition that he is made emperor, with only his brother as co-emperor. My children with Romanus will not be co-emperors. There will be no regents, and he will lead the empire as a true emperor. In the four years that have passed since Romanus took the throne, Michael has matured rapidly, and his training is complete. Agreed?"

Another bow. "Agreed."

"And as to my husband, he is to be presented your offer, and should he accept, then he should be provided the same provisions I have stipulated for his life in exile. But, should he not agree, and he challenges you for the throne, any agreement made here today concerning myself and my sons still stand. Agreed?"

John bowed deeply. "Agreed. Is that all?"

"Yes."

"Then, Eudokia, let us talk to Michael and put an end to the Diogenes line of ascension, and restore the Doukai line to its rightful place."

Leonardo da Vinci International Airport

Fiumicino, Italy

Present Day

Laura shivered as she stepped off her private jet and onto the tarmac. It was dark now, the day's heat already radiated off the concrete, and she was still dressed for the warmer Istanbul. She smiled as Giasson stepped out of an SUV with Vatican diplomatic markings.

"Laura, so good to see you again. I wish it were under better circumstances."

Laura gave him the traditional double-cheek kiss then a hug. "Good to see you too. How's the family?"

"Good. The girls keep growing. Soon they'll be old enough to hate me."

Laura chuckled. "Deep down, they'll still love their father." She became serious as they headed into the charter terminal. "Anything new from your end?"

Giasson shook his head. "Not much. We've determined that the courier that delivered the warning didn't work for the company the envelope indicated, and that they had no delivery in their system addressed to me at that time."

"Did you get them on camera?"

"Nothing useful. They seemed to know where every camera was, wore a hoodie with sunglasses, not to mention gloves. We couldn't even pull fingerprints from a door if we wanted to."

"Seems like they knew the place inside and out."

Giasson grunted as he opened the door for her. "I wouldn't be surprised if he worked ten feet away from me."

Laura eyed him. "You don't trust your own people?"

"You forget, one of my own was heavily involved with them. He lied to me for years."

Laura sighed. "That's the thing about groups like these. They can be anywhere, anyone. What precautions are you taking?"

"There's nothing more I can really do. I have to trust my people, and at the moment, we're not interfering. You are."

She pursed her lips. "The moment I step onto Vatican grounds, they might change their opinion on that."

Giasson frowned. "I had thought of that, however I don't want some cult dictating what I can and cannot do. The Vatican is sovereign territory and will not be dictated to by the Keepers of the One Truth."

"You do realize that when this is all over, there will likely be some interaction between the Keepers and the Vatican."

Giasson's eyes narrowed. "What do you mean?"

"The tablet, and perhaps a set of bones, will need to be stored in the Vault. The Keepers have the tablet, and tomorrow, they'll have the bones."

Giasson took her arm and stopped her. "Do you really think they'll find...*His* bones?"

Laura regarded the deeply religious man. "Let me say this. If the tablet tells the truth, then we'll find the bones there. But if the tablet is a hoax, don't you think they'd also have placed bones where the tablet says they should be found?" She resumed walking toward customs. "No matter what, mon ami, I have little doubt James will be finding something that will need explaining."

"God help us all."

Istanbul Police Headquarters

Istanbul, Turkey

"Palmer is in Rome."

Captain Demirel yanked his reading glasses off and looked up at his partner, Evren. "What?"

"She landed in Rome an hour ago."

"How is that possible? Why weren't we notified?"

"I made the request to add her to the watchlist, but someone screwed up. Her pilot filed a flight plan for Rome with an immediate departure, and the manifest was submitted but using her initials. Nobody caught it."

"What about the passport number? Shouldn't that have flagged her?"

"Apparently a typo that was corrected after they were in the air."

Demirel growled. "If that doesn't make her look guilty, I don't know what does." He leaned back. It didn't make sense. Why would she leave in such a manner? He had been convinced she was innocent in this matter and her husband likely was as well. The more he looked into these people, the more he realized they were upstanding citizens, well respected in their field, and extremely well connected.

These weren't criminals.

He was leaning toward believing the theory that Acton was being manipulated, extorted into taking the actions he had, but now? Her deception had him second-guessing everything.

"I want a warrant issued for her arrest."

"Sir?"

"You heard me."

Evren closed the office door. "You think she's involved?"

"After this, don't you?"

Evren shrugged. "Not really. Think about it. Were you going to let her leave?"

"No."

"And what would you have done if she had tried, and the system stopped her?"

"I would have arrested her."

"Exactly. Don't you think she knew that?"

Demirel regarded him for a moment. "And if she did?"

"You're an innocent woman of means, Western, Christian, in today's Turkey. You have a husband that has been kidnapped, possibly heading to Syria. What do you do? You don't stay here where you're powerless to do anything and might be arrested at any moment just because our system demands someone be blamed for every crime, even if they're innocent. You call your people and tell them to make it happen. I bet you she doesn't even know what was done to get her out."

Demirel pursed his lips. "You better be careful saying things like that. It's liable to get you dismissed from the force."

Evren shrugged. "It's not like the old days."

Demirel sighed. "No, it's definitely not. And you're right. If Ankara demands an arrest, she's the only one I can." He frowned. "She *was* the only one."

"What do we do now?"

"Only Professor Acton can answer the questions that need answering. Let's hope that he survives whatever is about to happen and we get a chance to interview him when this is all over."

"So, no arrest warrant?"

"No. Let her go for now. We might still have to issue one, but I doubt anyone will want to pursue extradition. She's safe. For the moment."

Approaching Syrian Coast

It had been a long time since Acton had laid on the deck of a boat and slept under the stars, and it was a lifestyle he could get used to. He understood the appeal. Getting away from civilization, the people, the noises, the smells. A return to nature without the hassles of camping. Lying under the stars as you bounced along the waves was almost primal.

And it could have been a hell of a good time if it weren't for the situation.

The vehicle they had transferred to was a boat, not another truck, and he and his captors had made it into international waters within minutes. This had set everyone at ease, including himself, for it meant he wasn't getting blown away by the Turkish Navy. But now they were approaching the Syrian coastline at four in the morning, and the possibility of capture and even death was a very real possibility.

This was perhaps the most dangerous part of his ordeal so far.

There were no guns on the boat. He had watched as everything from handguns to knives were tossed overboard. There would be no defending themselves against any Syrian security.

"What do we do if we're captured?" he asked Esposito.

Esposito faced him. "Tell them nothing about why we are here, just that we kidnapped you in Istanbul and forced you to steal the tablet. You don't know what it is, and you don't know where it is."

Acton's eyes narrowed. "Wait, you don't have it with you?"

"No. It's been handed off. We don't need the tablet to get where we're going, only the words inscribed on it."

It made sense. Even he wouldn't have brought it with them if this were a sanctioned dig. The tablet was an ancient artifact that needed to be properly preserved, not hauled around the world unnecessarily. He had little doubt their motivations were different. They didn't want it falling into anyone's hands. A photo meant nothing. It could be written off as a forgery with little challenge. "So, you want me to rat you out."

Esposito stared at him, puzzled. "Excuse me?"

Acton shook his head. "Nothing. I mean, you want me to tell them the truth, that you kidnapped me. Doesn't that kind of seal your fate?"

"Our fate was sealed the day we took our vows. Dying for the cause is our greatest honor. But when you are set free, you must complete the mission."

Acton's eyebrows shot up his forehead. "Are you kidding me?"

"We must determine if this is a hoax, and you are the best man for the job. If we are captured, you must promise me that you will complete our mission."

"How? They'll arrest me for sure if I try."

"You are a resourceful man, Professor. I've followed your career since our first encounter, and I know if there is anyone who can find a way, it is you." Esposito leaned closer, tapping Acton's chest. "Remember, your wife's life is at stake here."

Acton regarded him. "If you're dead—"

"Your deal isn't with me, it's with the Keepers of the One Truth. I merely occupy a position. If I die, someone will replace me. If all my men die here today, others will contact you. The entire organization knows the agreement we made. You must complete the mission for your wife to be safe."

Acton sighed. "Fine. But I have a better plan."

"What's that?"

"Let's just not get caught."

Esposito laughed, slapping Acton on the arm. "I like you, Professor. I think under different circumstances, we could be friends."

"I'm not so sure about that."

The captain motioned for them to get down, and everyone crouched as the engine was cut, their momentum carrying them to shore.

"You'd be surprised how much we have in common. Did you know that I too am an academic? I teach history."

Acton stared at the man, stunned. "You teach? I thought you were roaming around, looking for threats."

"We all have lives, Professor. Yes, some roam about, like you say, but the best way to find out about things that might threaten the Church is to live a fulfilling life, to talk to people, to interact, to converse with academics in the field who might encounter the next threat. How do you think we found out about the tablet? We had people monitoring the social media accounts of archaeologists and their students. How do you think we recognized its significance? Because we had people educated in Biblical Hebrew. We're not mindless drones. We're people of faith and education, willing to die to protect what we believe in."

The boat bumped onto shore and everyone climbed down the ladder and into the water before pushing the boat back. Acton followed his captors onto the shore, his head on a swivel for trouble. If they encountered Syrian security, he was hitting the ground immediately. There was no way in hell he was risking his life by attempting to evade the authorities. But it would mean returning later for another attempt if Esposito were to be believed and Laura's life was still at risk.

He stared up at the stars as he sloshed to shore.

Please God, let us all get through this, for Laura's sake.

Down the coast, at least several miles away, he could see lights, but in the immediate vicinity they were lit only by the night sky. He nearly pissed his pants as headlights flashed ahead, but as they cycled on and off three times, he breathed easier, realizing it was a signal from whoever they were meeting.

They raced across the beach and toward the vehicle, and moments later, without a word exchanged, they were in the back of a cloth-sided delivery truck, heading away from the shore.

An anticlimactic end to his journey.

Just the way he liked it.

Yet this wasn't the end. If they had landed where he suspected they would, they still had hours of driving to get to the location indicated on the tablet, and in a country like Syria, that could mean countless roadblocks or worse.

This was far from over.

Beirut-Rafic Hariri International Airport

Beirut, Lebanon

Leather smiled broadly at a man he hadn't seen in years. When in the SAS, one of his missions had taken him into Lebanon in pursuit of a terrorist responsible for killing several British citizens in Jordan. The Lebanese had quietly cooperated, assigning Farez Yassin as their liaison. A friendship had been kindled, and Leather had kept in touch with the man over the years, offering him a job in his firm if he were even interested.

Yassin wasn't.

He was committed to rebuilding his country, though all recent reports Leather had read suggested it was a losing battle. Lebanon was heading backward, not forward.

Yassin smiled, grabbing Leather by both shoulders and planting a kiss on each cheek. "How are you doing, my old friend?"

Leather returned the gesture—when in Rome. "I'm doing well. How's the family?"

"Good! Good! My wife, she wants to meet you, but I said you have no time. Very busy man."

"I am, but pass on my respects to her. You have what we need?"

"Not with me, but I will. It's not wise for you to be stopped in a vehicle filled with weapons. My supplier will meet us closer to the border."

Leather slapped Yassin on the back. "This is why I want you working for me. Always thinking ahead." They climbed into a large SUV that had seen better days, much like the entire country. "So, do you think we'll have any trouble?"

Yassin shrugged. "If we do, I talk us out of it. You've all got your passports and visas?"

"Yes."

"And cash?"

"Enough to grease every palm from here to the border."

"Then I anticipate no problems. I suggest you lean back and enjoy the ride. Get some rest if you can. If you need me to get you into Syria, I doubt it's to see the sights."

Leather grunted. "You wouldn't believe me if I told you."

Northeast of Homs, Syria

Dawson spoke flawless Russian. When he started his career, he had chosen several languages to learn. Arabic and Farsi were the obvious choices at the time since the world felt Islam would be the problem, but he had listened to his father who had assured him that sooner or later, the Russians would be a problem again.

And the old man had been right.

Which meant he could pass himself off as Wagner if necessary, as could several of the others in their vehicle. They were en route to Acton's expected destination. Last night, after receiving their new orders, they had packed up their gear and loaded it in their SUV hidden behind the walls of the compound they were using, then waited for dawn.

Driving at night was slow on the roads around here, especially the backroads they'd be taking, but it necessitated headlights, which meant they could be seen for miles. At this hour, with the sun just coming up, it was early enough that most casual observers were still asleep, and the roads were sufficiently revealed that headlights weren't necessary.

It also meant any roadblocks were manned by the tired nightshift, not the bright-eyed, newly arrived dayshift.

Langley was in his ear, guiding them through the gauntlet, and so far they had managed to avoid any roadblocks or other problems, though the route was slow. They had no idea when Acton would be arriving. It could be any minute now, it could be tomorrow. There was just no way to know. Langley had every eye in the sky available scouring every route leading to the ultimate destination, but it would be like finding a needle in a haystack where the needle had a roof over its head.

They would only know he was there when he climbed out of whatever got him there.

And Dawson wanted to be there before that happened, so they could pre-position themselves to take out the hostiles without risking Acton. He had to assume it was a small party to attract less attention. They were six, and if the enemy was the same or less, they could drop all six and end this. That was the ideal solution, though unfortunately, things rarely worked out ideally. They were in disputed territory. Syrian troops were everywhere, Wagner was as well, not to mention elements of what remained of ISIS and various other factions. It was anarchy outside of the cities, and a bunch of Americans were juicy targets.

But a bunch of Americans passing themselves off as Russians? Not as much.

"Zero-One, hold your position, over."

Dawson geared down and came to a halt slowly so as not to create a cloud of dust. "Holding, Control. What's the situation?"

"We've got a Wagner vehicle approaching a crossroads ahead. Stand by while we see which direction they take."

"Do our old ROEs still apply?"

"What were your old ROEs?"

"Engage when engaged only."

"Negative. New ROEs are to engage if deemed necessary for the success of the mission."

Dawson smiled at the others. "Confirmed, Control. ROEs are to engage if deemed necessary for the success of the mission."

Leroux cursed. "Zero-One, they've turned and are now heading in your direction."

"Any chance they'll turn off this road?"

"Negative. There are no side roads. They are coming directly for you. ETA three minutes."

"Control, to confirm, we have unknown number of Wagner hostiles approaching our position with no opportunity to evade. It is my assessment that this constitutes a risk to mission success. Does Control concur?"

"Control concurs. You are cleared to engage."

Dawson gave a thumbs-up to the others as fist bumps were exchanged. "Copy that, Control. Preparing to engage. Any estimates as to how many we're facing?"

"It's an up-armored SUV. No more than eight."

"Copy that. Keep us posted as needed. Zero-One, out." He turned to the others. "Atlas, break out the Gustaf and find a good position. Everyone else, find good firing positions. I want all arcs covered with no casualties. I'd rather have a sustained fight than a brief one with a round in someone's ass."

Niner grinned at Atlas. "He's talking to you."

"I'm going to play broken down driver." Dawson popped the hood. "When I drop the hood, Atlas, take out their vehicle, everyone else clean your arc then assist. Understood?"

"Yes, Sergeant Major!"

"Good. Let's kill some Rooskies."

Lebanon/Syria Border

Leather peered through the binoculars at the border to Syria from Lebanon. They had seen several patrols over the past hour along with light traffic across the small border crossing in the middle of nowhere. The guards appeared bored, though whenever a superior arrived in a vehicle, they were on alert, all movements crisp and brisk.

They were poorly paid conscripts who didn't want to be there.

The perfect soldier for their purposes.

"Ready?" asked Yassin.

Leather nodded. "Yup."

"Good. I'll do the talking, you hand over the money. I assume your Arabic is still up to snuff?"

"My Arabic is perfect," replied Leather in Arabic.

Yassin laughed. "If you say so. Like I said, keep your mouth shut, but listen for how much to hand over. We don't want to flash more than necessary."

"Understood."

They headed back to their vehicle parked just off the road behind some heavy brush and climbed in. Within minutes, Yassin had them rolling up to the Lebanese side of the border crossing. They were given the standard warnings then waved through after a palmed wad of cash was exchanged. It was clear this was a well-used route for smuggling and other nefarious business.

He just hoped the next side of the exchange went as smoothly.

"I don't recognize this guy," said Yassin as they approached, a guard holding up his hand, ordering them to stop.

"Is that a problem?"

"Let's hope not. If it is, let's try non-lethal, understood?"

Leather unclipped his seatbelt, but kept it in position so as to not raise any suspicions. "Understood."

"Good morning, my friend," said Yassin with a broad smile. He held out his papers along with a bulging wad of cash tucked inside. "My friends and I have business in your country. We'll be back before the day is out."

The man opened the passport and frowned as he held up the cash. "And what's this? A bribe?"

Yassin laughed. "No, nothing of the sort. I guess I should have explained before handing it over. My business is with a cousin on my wife's side. I don't trust him. I want you to hold on to that for me until I get back. In fact, I have some more that needs to be kept safe, if you're amenable. I would pay you for your services, of course." Yassin held his hand out behind him, four fingers displayed. Leather retrieved 400,000 Lebanese pounds, about $250, and pressed it into Yassin's hand. Yassin handed the large stack over. "Could you hang on to this for me? I just don't trust the man. You can take whatever holding fee you want out of that. Let's consider it insurance."

The soldier eyed Yassin skeptically then tossed the papers and cash onto the ground as he stepped back, unslinging his AKM assault rifle. Leather drew his taser and leaned forward, unloading thousands of volts into the man's chest as the other two doors of their vehicle opened and his men poured out, taking down the second guard without a shot fired.

"Tie them up and gag them," ordered Leather. "And get the papers and as much of the money as you can. The last thing we need is interest being paid because they think there's a pot of gold somewhere."

Yassin waved his hand. "No. Just find my papers. Leave the money where it is."

Leather eyed him. "Why?"

"We'll take them with us then leave them a few kilometers from here. They'll free themselves eventually, or we will on our way back, but I want it to look like they had a big pay day and abandoned their post. That way their superiors will think they went AWOL instead of getting captured."

Leather chuckled. "I like the way you think." He turned to the others. "You heard the man. Get them in the back and let's get the hell out of here before one of the patrols returns." He climbed into the passenger seat. "Now let's hope our Lebanese witnesses don't rat us out."

Northeast of Homs, Syria

Dawson leaned over the engine, his shirt tied around his waist revealing not only his chiseled physique but the fact he had nothing to hide. The only piece of equipment he had from the waist up was his earpiece, tucked out of sight in his ear canal.

He wasn't a primary in this fight, he was the decoy.

"Thirty seconds," whispered Leroux in his ear, and Dawson suppressed a smile.

"You don't need to whisper, just don't shout."

"Sorry, Zero-One. I had a rough night."

"You sound a little off."

"Here they come. Fifty meters."

Dawson didn't need the warning. He could hear the engine of the SUV approaching for the past two minutes, echoing among the rocks of the sparse, dry landscape. He kept his back to them as the tires rolled over the packed dirt, the distinctive sound allowing him to judge their

208

speed and demeanor. It was a gentle easing off the gas, no sense of urgency detected.

"Twenty meters directly behind you."

Doors opened.

"All four doors opening. Four men stepping out, one from each door. All armed. Three covering, passenger leaning on doorframe."

"Hey, you, car trouble?" asked the man in Arabic, but with a thick Russian accent.

Dawson forced a smile and slowly turned, replying in Russian. "I'm out of oil. I must have cracked the pan on these shit roads."

The man smiled. "You're Russian?"

"Born and bred. St. Petersburg. You?"

"Volgograd. What are you doing out here?"

"Let's just say I'm on business that interests Mother Russia."

The man laughed, stepping away from the safety of his reinforced door. "Aren't we all. You're alone?"

"I wasn't. My partner went back in our transport to get some help." Dawson patted the SUV. "I didn't want to leave this baby out here alone. There'd be nothing of her left by the time we got back."

"That's true. These bastards will steal anything. Are you armed?"

Dawson gestured toward the cabin. "I've got a rifle and a Makarov plus plenty of ammo. And I can shoot. That usually makes the difference."

The man roared. "I like this guy. Balls like a bear!"

Dawson grinned then slammed the hood shut. An 84mm round from a Carl Gustaf recoilless rifle streaked from behind a large boulder to his right as disciplined shots took out all four targets simultaneously. They collapsed to the ground as the round slammed into their vehicle. It erupted in a terrific explosion that would, unfortunately, stain the brightening sky and draw attention. The safer play might have been to leave the Gustaf out of it, but they couldn't risk that there were more inside that would then engage.

This was over.

And as if to prove him right, a fifth man rolled out of the rear door and onto the ground, writhing in agony for a few moments before falling silent.

"Strip them of anything valuable. Let's make this look like a hit by a local faction."

His men went to work as Dawson pulled their SUV around the wreckage, positioning them for a rapid exit. Five men were dead in an ambush with no hopes of defending themselves. There were times when he might be conflicted about that, but not today. Not only were these Russians clearly the enemy once again, these were soldiers for hire who would brutally murder anyone they considered a threat, including his team.

No sympathy.

And no time.

"Let's get a wiggle on, ladies! I want to put as much distance between us and this as possible."

Operations Center 3, CIA Headquarters

Langley, Virginia

Leroux popped another Tylenol then downed it with a mouthful of water. He checked the dosage on the bottle then doubled up. Even a few more hours sleep after another good soaking in the shower hadn't helped his head, though had apparently helped those around him. Kane had called about ten minutes ago and just laughed at him then said he was going back to bed.

I'm going to kill him.

"Ugh, I'm never drinking again."

"I call bullshit on that," said Child. "The next time that smokin' hot girlfriend of yours asks you out for drinks, you know you're there."

Tong's eyebrow shot up as she turned in her seat. "That's your boss' girlfriend you're talking about there. Show some respect."

Therrien chimed in. "For him or her?"

"Both, but mostly her."

211

Child spun in his chair. "How's complimenting her not showing respect?"

"Yes, I'm sure she wants some pimply-faced geek barely out of puberty commenting on how attractive she is."

Child dropped a foot, halting his spin. "Hey, I can assure you I finished puberty years ago." His eyes narrowed. "Hey, wait a minute. Why is it okay for you to insult me, but it's not okay for me to compliment her?"

"Would you say it to her face?"

"Huh?"

"Would you say it to her face?"

Therrien snorted. "*He* probably would."

Child shrugged. "I probably would, but I've been told I have no filter."

Tong shook her head. "No sense either. And I apologize for insulting you. You just pushed my buttons today."

Child frowned. "Yeah, I guess I'm sorry. I'm just used to talking to my friends, and they're all my age. Everyone here is so old, I don't know what I'm allowed to say."

This garnered him the ire of the entire room and Leroux saved the kid before someone authorized a drone strike on him.

"Okay, okay. Randy, back to work before you get yourself added to the Kill List. Everyone else, remember the dumbass stuff you said when you were his age. None of us were angels"—several women cleared their throats—"especially us guys. Let's just remember the venue."

Child leaned forward, lowering his voice. "Sorry, boss. I didn't mean to insult Sherrie."

Leroux dismissed the apology. "Don't worry about it. Trust me, I've heard her say worse about other women."

Child stared at him. "You are a God to me."

"I've got something!" exclaimed Tong, hopping in her chair as she tapped at her keyboard then stared at the displays. Leroux rose, his head pounding, and he reached out to steady himself.

"What are we looking at?"

"The first vehicle to come even close to our target coordinates."

Leroux cursed. "You mean Acton's there already?"

"It would appear so."

"Shit. ETA on Delta?"

"One hour."

"And Leather?"

"Thirty minutes."

He pursed his lips. "Any sign of activity in the area?"

"Affirmative. We have a Syrian unit two miles to the west, about twenty regulars accompanied by a Wagner unit. Looks like four to six men."

"Where are they headed?"

"Nowhere for the moment. Looks like a pee break."

"Good. Let's just hope nothing draws their attention to the east."

Kotyaion, Eastern Roman Empire

AD 1072

Romanus sat in his cell broken, defeated, and betrayed. He had returned from his defeat at Manzikert, but had received word of the betrayal by the Doukai family through a message from Eudokia passed on by Alexander. It was a heart-wrenching confession as to what she had agreed to, but there had been no choice.

The Doukai family had no honor, and they would have killed her and anyone who stood in their way. He understood why she had made the agreement she did—she had saved all their lives to give him an opportunity to fight back.

And he did, yet he had lost. His forces were simply too weakened, and too many no longer believed he was emperor. He had been forced to surrender and commit to the agreement his wife had negotiated, his safety guaranteed by the traitor Andronicus Doukas, the arrangement ratified by the Senate.

He was resigned to his fate of a life of relative solitude. He had come to think of the past five years as a bonus provided to him by God. He should have died years ago, yet his beloved wife had saved him. Yes, for her own purposes, though ultimately, he still believed, for the betterment of the empire. He had shown them what could be done with a well-trained citizen army of sufficient numbers. He just prayed that his defeats weren't misinterpreted as proof his theory didn't work.

He had lost because he had pressed too soon. Another year, perhaps two, to build their numbers, and he would have easily won. He could have claimed the territory necessary to prove whether the tablet was legitimate. Yet he had failed, and he realized now that his lack of patience was the sin that had ultimately led to his defeat, and his failure to save Christianity from what he had to assume was a hoax.

For he lived. He had survived a vicious defeat. He had been spared by the sultan and treated like a king after the ritual humiliation. He had survived the failed attempts to regain his throne.

Though something had gone wrong.

In the middle of the night, he had been hauled from his new home and blindfolded, and now occupied a small, filthy cell, vermin his only company. He had no idea what was going on, though it certainly violated the agreement made with those who had usurped his throne.

He feared the worst, and expected that the next time the door opened, he would be led to his execution. If that were to be the case then so be it. He would die an honorable man, for he wasn't the one that had violated the agreement. His only regret would be not seeing his beloved Eudokia one last time, nor his sons.

He just prayed that something similar wasn't happening to his family elsewhere in the empire.

Footfalls echoed on the other side of the metal door and he pushed to his feet, making himself as presentable as possible. While those who had abducted him might have no honor, he did, and would face whatever was to come with dignity, for he was a Roman, and Romans were proud, courageous, and unwavering in the face of their enemies.

Yet why did his knees shake? If he died here today, he was certain he would be embraced by God and welcomed into the Kingdom of Heaven. But for some reason, he had doubts. It had to be the tablet. It remained unresolved, the words written on it neither proven nor disproven. Yet the entire episode had shaken his faith, and perhaps that was what troubled him now.

Would God forgive him for his doubt?

And what if the tablet were true, and he had spent his life worshipping a false prophet? Would God forgive him for worshipping a man as His son? Would he be condemned to eternal damnation for violating the most important of the Commandments?

A key hit the lock and he drew a deep breath, steeling for what was to come. The door opened and two guards stepped inside, each grabbing him by an arm. He was led out of his cell and up a narrow set of stairs then through a long corridor before being shown into a large room with a chair in the center. The guards shoved him into it then bound his hands and feet before strapping his head to the raised back.

It was this that had his heart racing. He could understand the hands and feet, but why his head? What did they have planned for him? A door opened at the far end of the room and people filed in, dressed in their finest. They were too far away and the light too dim for him to recognize anyone, but as they neared, rage ignited in his stomach.

John Doukas.

He should have known the bastard was behind this. Only a Doukai would betray an agreement approved by the Senate, the sitting emperor, and the clergy that had agreed to take him into exile. He glared at the man as he approached, a smirk on his face, and it was that smirk that had him terrified.

What did they have planned for him? A simple execution wouldn't merit a smirk. Even John would know death was something he didn't fear. A smirk suggested something far more sinister, and it had to be related to why his head was strapped into place.

He breathed slightly easier when the three bishops who had helped craft the agreement approached, all with concerned and puzzled expressions. It suggested to him that they too were in the dark as to what was going on. The party was small, perhaps ten people within sight, another dozen or so guards standing at the far end in the shadows.

A fire flared as coals were poked, but he paid it no mind.

The bishop of Chalkedon turned to John. "Caesar John, for what purpose have you called us all here, and why is he restrained like this? He is supposed to be under our care, in exile, as agreed, treated with the respect he deserves."

John stepped forward, never taking his eyes off Romanus. "New evidence has come to light that requires an adjustment to the agreement."

"What new evidence? We haven't been shown anything."

"You don't need to be. You are merely religious leaders. Those in power have reviewed the evidence, have concluded it is genuine, and have decided upon the punishment."

"At least tell us the nature of this evidence."

"Letters between Romanus Diogenes and his loyal supporters, plotting his escape from your care, then his plans for retaking the throne."

"That's a lie!" cried Romanus. "There have been no such letters!"

John held up a sheaf of parchment, shaking the pages in Romanus' face. "*You* lie! I have the proof here. They may not be in your handwriting, but they are your words. Obviously you have been dictating to someone what you wanted written. But we've been intercepting your correspondence, and all those involved have now been arrested and will be put to the sword."

"But it's a lie! I've done no such thing! Anyone you kill is innocent!" Romanus turned to the bishops. "You must believe me. I have honored the agreement. I have corresponded only with my wife and closest family, and nothing has ever been said such as what he claims. He is lying. You must believe me."

The bishop consulted with the others in whispered tones then turned to John. "This is most unusual. We have monitored all his communications as per the agreement, and nothing has left the monastery other than letters as he has described."

John dismissed the bishop's observations with a wave of his hand. "As I said, he's dictating the letters to someone, bypassing you entirely.

But his treachery was discovered, and now it is time to deliver his punishment."

"And what punishment is that?"

"He is to be blinded. Immediately."

Everyone gathered gasped, and Romanus slumped in the chair as the fire flared again, a red-hot poker pulled from the coals. "No! You can't do this!"

The bishop rushed between Romanus and the beast approaching with the poker. "This is unacceptable! It is an affront before God! Oaths were sworn, agreements signed in the name of God!"

The other two bishops formed a wall between Romanus and the approaching man, but the guards at the far end of the room hurried forward, hustling the three out of the way.

They wouldn't be his saviors today.

Romanus wrenched his head toward John. "John, please, you must believe me. I did nothing such as you have described. I'm being set up. You have to believe me."

The poker approached, the man holding it no longer in focus, the red and orange glowing tip all that he could see.

"Please, John! Have mercy!"

John stepped closer, bent down, then whispered in Romanus' ear. "There is no mercy for a traitor such as yourself."

"I'm no traitor! I swear it! I have upheld the agreement! I'm being set up!"

John sneered at him, lowering his voice even further as his hot breath blew on Romanus' ear. "I know. I'm the one who set you up. And once you are blinded, no man in the empire will ever follow you."

Tears rolled down Romanus' cheeks as the man carrying the hot poker stopped behind John. "Please," he whispered. "I beg of you."

John stared into his eyes, and Romanus saw nothing but pure evil. "You and your family's claim to the throne is over. The Diogenes family is finished." He stepped back, making way for the man who would deliver the punishment, and Romanus' heart slammed as he saw not hatred in the beast's eyes, but uncertainty. He held out the poker, aiming it straight for Romanus' eye, then changed position, bringing it in at an angle before stopping yet again.

He has no clue what he's doing!

Romanus yanked at his bonds, shoving one shoulder out then the other in an attempt to loosen the restraints holding his head. He couldn't let this amateur deliver the blinding. An arm came loose and he yanked it free. He reached over to free his other arm when John took action.

"Restrain him!"

The guards rushed forward and one grabbed his free arm. He continued his struggle, and it took five men to finally restrain him, one of them placing his shield on his arms, another on his chest, restricting his breathing. Two men gripped his head and held it in place, though he still managed to move it slightly as the poker approached. As the tip pressed against his eyeball, he roared in agony, momentarily jerking his head free. He was restrained again, the poker reapplied, and it took a moment for him to realize the blood-curdling scream that echoed through the room was his own.

The incompetent fool, for he was incompetent as Romanus could still see, moved in for a third attempt on the same eye as the bishops begged for the torture to stop. John ignored them, the wall of guards preventing any interference, and as the poker pressed against him once again, this time piercing the eye socket completely, the Good Lord granted him mercy, and he passed out from the pain, hoping to never awake.

I'm sorry I ever doubted.

Suspected Burial Site

South of Homs, Syria

Present Day

Acton climbed out of the back of the truck that had carried them from the coast. It was hours of discomfort accompanied by a little bit of agony, but judging from the landscape, they had reached their destination. Southern Syria. If they had, then they were farther south than Romanus had ever reached, which would explain why the mystery of the tablet had never been solved.

The location was intriguing. It was far enough south that it would take years of campaigning for the Byzantines to reach, but also close enough to Jerusalem that it was believable the bones could have been taken from the original burial site to here in a reasonable amount of time with little difficulty.

It lent credibility to the tablet's authenticity, but also to it being an eleventh-century hoax.

He stared at the rockface in front of them that stretched in either direction. The tablet had referred to Emesa, the pre-Islamic name for Homs, now a city of over half a million to the north, and the rock formations due south of it. From the stone climbing on either side, gently to the north, steeper to the south, this would be the first gorge in the formation referred to.

"And this is the exact midpoint?" he asked Esposito.

Esposito shrugged. "I don't know, Professor. These are the coordinates you gave us."

Acton faced south. "Then this is the location."

"I don't see anything."

Acton chuckled. "You'd make a terrible archaeologist. If it were sitting out in the open, it would have been found long ago and looted. The fact we can't see it is a good thing. There's not a lot of activity in this area, and there never was historically. That's not to say someone didn't stumble upon the cave we're looking for, but it reduces the likelihood. Obviously, somebody did, if those who hid the bones knew where it was."

"Or this is the hoax we know it to be."

Acton decided not to argue. "How about we look? Let's spread out along this ridge. Remember, the tablet said the midpoint, but they didn't exactly have precise measuring back then. According to the tablet it will be about twenty meters up behind an outcropping. Things could have changed, however, over two thousand years. Let's just keep our eyes open."

Acton stood, slowly examining the rockface as the others spread out. They needed time to do this properly, the one thing they didn't have. More manpower would be nice too. He stopped. The tablet referred to an ancient burial site in the hillside. If that were the case, then there had to be a way to reach it without scaling the rocks from handhold to handhold. Ancient religious figures, families, mourners, all could have made the journey. Even after 2000 years there should still be some sign of a pathway, perhaps mostly eroded away, but still there nonetheless.

He stepped farther back, slowly scanning from left to right, searching for anything that suggested a pathway leading from the ground they now stood on to about sixty feet up.

And he spotted something.

He jogged about a hundred yards to the left of their current position and kicked at the rockface. There was an outcropping, barely two feet across at its widest, that slowly rose upward. Two thousand years ago, it just might have been double that width or more—a comfortable climb to a tomb.

"Over here!" he shouted. "This might be what we're looking for. Just let me test it for stability."

The others gathered as he carefully made his way up, testing each step with a stomp of his shoe. As he got higher, he began searching for handholds as well, the drop not high enough to kill him yet, but definitely high enough to leave him gravely injured.

He stopped. Ahead, the ledge he was on was barely six inches wide. Enough for a toehold at best. The segment was only about four feet, but there was no margin for error. He drew a deep breath and extended his right foot tentatively. He pressed it tight against the rockface then put some weight on it.

It held.

He shuffled forward, then repeated the process half a dozen times before reaching the next wider segment. He leaned against the cliff face for a few moments, steadying his nerves. He had expected there might be some rock climbing, but he hadn't exactly been asked for an equipment list, nor had he been in a state of mind to offer one. When he had described where they were headed, however, he would have expected his captors to plan ahead.

"What's the problem? Get moving! We don't have any time to waste!" shouted Esposito from below.

Acton glanced down at him. "If you think you can do better, you're welcome to come up here."

Esposito tapped his watch. "Time is a commodity not to be wasted, Professor. Not in this part of the world."

Acton growled but continued, and was pleased to find most of the rest of the ledge was wide enough to walk along with relative ease. He reached a larger outcropping and found the path didn't continue past it. This had to be it. He carefully surveyed the area, but found no opening in the rockface. If this wasn't the location, then it must be farther up the hill, and the path to it long eroded away.

He stepped as close to the edge as he dared, then took another look as the sun continued to rise. And a smile slowly spread at the shadow cast by part of the stone in front of him. A nearly perfect semi-circle. He hurried back to the rock and examined the edge creating the shadow. It was a separate stone.

It was a sealing stone.

Time had worn it away, but it had done its job, preserving whatever was behind it from man and beast, wind and rain.

And it terrified him.

Everything the tablet had stated so far had been true, if what lay beyond this stone were indeed a burial site. Was he about to disprove the greatest story ever told? And what would those below him do if he did?

You'll be dead in a heartbeat.

They wouldn't hesitate to kill him to prevent the truth from getting out. He would face that problem later. For now, he was trying to save Laura's life. He leaned over the ledge. "I've found it!"

Excited utterances from below didn't sound happy. They, like him, obviously were hoping there would be nothing here.

"We're going to need some equipment to break through the sealing stone, however. Do you have anything?"

"Yes. We'll be up in a few minutes."

Acton decided it was time to think. He sat with his back against the sealing stone and watched the sun slowly climb in the sky as those below got busy. He stared all the way up and wondered if his friends at the CIA or in Delta were actually watching. It was a distinct possibility. He gave a wave, wondering if they could see him. Laura would have contacted Kane, he was certain of that. She also would have figured out the general GPS coordinates like he had. Between her and Reading, they would have guessed that he would eventually show up here, so if the CIA was so inclined, they would be watching.

But could they put people in to get him out?

And if they did, would he have already fulfilled his obligations to the Keepers, or would they be killed before he had the chance to save his wife?

Operations Center 3, CIA Headquarters

Langley, Virginia

Leroux rose as Morrison entered the operations center. Their boss examined the various feeds on the main display as he made his way to the center of the room where Leroux's station was located.

"Sitrep?"

"We've confirmed it's Acton and we assume his abductors." Leroux turned to Tong. "Show him the clip."

Tong tapped a few keys and the clip showing Acton waving at them appeared.

Morrison's eyes narrowed. "That's satellite footage, isn't it? Not drone?"

"Yes, sir."

"Then how—"

"We assume he's being cheeky, sir. He's hoping we're watching because of past history."

Morrison grunted. "One of these days we won't be. Delta?"

"Delta is forty-five out and Leather's team is fifteen. But there's a problem. Several, in fact."

"I don't like problems."

"Well, you're really not going to like this. Leather's team captured the border guards when they—"

"Why the hell would they do that?"

"The guard drew on them. They had no choice. They tied them up and dropped them off a few minutes from their post. A regular patrol, however, found the post abandoned so have put out a call. Troops are moving into the area to search for what they're reporting as AWOL soldiers."

Morrison sat in a nearby chair and Leroux thankfully dropped into his own, his body still protesting being there. "That's good, isn't it? It means they don't know what really happened."

"Yes and no. It's good like you say, but it's bad in that scores of troops are entering the area, cutting off their primary route of escape. There's no way Leather's team is getting out the way they came in."

Morrison pursed his lips, exhaling loudly through his nose. "And there's more?"

"Yes. Delta was forced to take out a group of five Wagner personnel—"

"Good."

"—and their bodies have been discovered. Wagner is mobilizing everything in the area. It cuts off any escape to the east, north, or south."

Morrison closed his eyes for a moment. "Just once, just once…" He exhaled. "Okay, what do you recommend?"

"We need to put some airpower on standby. The USS Iwo Jima is offshore. She could put an Osprey in there for extraction, and four SuperCobras for ground support. It would at least give them all a fighting chance. They might be able to rescue Acton, but there's no way in hell they're getting out of there alive."

"This is going to need approval." Morrison pushed to his feet. "I'll let you know."

"Oh, and one more thing."

"Ugh. There's more?"

"Professor Palmer is asking for a feed to our coverage on her husband."

"You told her we have it?"

"No, but she's a smart lady. She knows we're capable."

"Fine. Declassified grade only."

"We'll dumb it down, sir."

Morrison left the room, muttering to himself about retiring, and everyone grinned at each other.

"Sonya, would you take care of the feed for Palmer?"

"I'm on it."

Leroux's head collapsed onto his desk. "Kill me now."

Child's chair stopped spinning behind him. "Umm, boss?"

"What?"

"We've got activity."

"Where?"

"At Acton's position. Someone's approaching."

Suspected Burial Site
South of Homs, Syria

Acton was a little miffed. It turned out his captors' contact had come prepared. He had an assortment of climbing equipment as well as rigging for raising and lowering supplies. Acton had risked his neck needlessly. When he had asked why no one had said anything, he didn't like the answer any better than the revelation.

"You never asked."

Prybars and rock hammers were hard at work on the sealing stone. He preferred a more delicate approach, but time was of the essence as Esposito had indicated, and he had a sense that once inside, nobody but himself would be concerned with proper protocols. Whatever they found would be taken by the Keepers back to Rome.

Or worse.

A vehicle approaching had everyone stopping. Esposito stepped to the edge and waved, a greeting shouted in Arabic.

"Visitors?" asked Acton.

"Fellow Keepers. They've been waiting nearby for word that the tomb actually exists."

"You already had people here? Then why are we here?"

"Because you're the expert. Besides, they never would have found it. It was your expertise that got us this far."

Acton frowned. "Yay me."

A man climbed up one of the ropes they had rigged and hugs were exchanged with the others.

"We'll speak English for the benefit of Professor Acton," said Esposito. "Did you bring what we need?"

"More than enough, I'm sure." The new arrival handed over a small package then nodded toward the sealing stone. "This should make quick work of that."

Esposito smiled. "Good thinking." He tossed the package to one of the others then gestured to the ropes. "Professor, I suggest we head down below."

"Why?"

"We're going to blow the entrance."

Acton's eyes rolled back as he sighed. "If you use too much, you'll destroy whatever is inside. If you're not careful, you could take half the hill down on top of it."

"I'm willing to take that risk if it saves us hours of work."

Acton shrugged as he grabbed the rope and swung over the side. "It's your choice. Just don't get mad at me when things go horribly wrong."

Operations Center 3, CIA Headquarters

Langley, Virginia

"Looks like they're friendlies."

Tong grunted at Child's observation. "That's a matter of opinion. Friendly to the Keepers, not to the professor."

"Got me there. At least they didn't come in with guns-a-blazin'."

"What the hell are they doing?" Leroux peered at the live image as the small ledge they had been working on was cleared. Something had been tossed and some work done at an angle they couldn't see clearly, and now everyone was evacuating. "Oh shit, they're blowing it." He snapped his fingers. "Let's get some more eyes on that Syrian-Wagner unit nearby. When this thing blows, they're within earshot, even if it isn't visible."

"On it," replied Tong who then retasked some of the team as Leroux refocused his attention on the hostiles in the region. A flash from Acton's position lasted only a moment, and they had no audio, but the reaction from the Syrian position was instantaneous.

Those on the ground turned south.

Leroux checked the feed of Acton's position and found it obscured with dust from the detonation, the fine particulate slowly dissipating, and while the initial explosion might not have been visible, the aftermath likely was, giving the Syrians an exact location for the source of what they had just heard.

"That doesn't look good," muttered Child as Leroux frowned.

The Syrians and Russians were rushing toward their vehicles, and half their number were soon heading south to Acton's position.

Less than ten minutes away.

Suspected Burial Site

South of Homs, Syria

Acton cursed as he slowly rose, debris from the far too large blast scattered everywhere, the windshield of their vehicle pockmarked. An argument broke out among Esposito and the new arrival responsible for the detonation, but Acton ignored it. These idiots had just set off a blast that could be heard for miles, and the dust they had thrown up could be seen just as far.

Anyone with a gun and curiosity was heading here.

And there was no time to waste. He grabbed one of the ropes and tested it. It still held. He climbed up the rockface then rolled onto the ledge. The sealing stone was no more, the blast effective—he just hoped it wasn't too effective. If what they were looking for was directly on the other side, then it could have been destroyed in the explosion.

As he approached, checking above for any loose rocks that might fall on him, he was of mixed feelings. He didn't want this responsibility. He wanted to just go home and hold his wife, safe with the knowledge the

Keepers weren't coming after them. If the blast had destroyed everything, then there would be nothing to find, nothing to explain. Yet the scientist in him still wanted to solve the mystery. Was the tablet real? Were His bones inside? And if they were, then did it mean He was just a he?

He closed his eyes for a moment as the bickering continued below, out of sight. He said a silent prayer, begging for forgiveness should what he discover cause anyone pain or harm, then opened his eyes and stepped through. Light poured through the entrance, revealing a small forecourt with several tunnels branching off from it. It appeared to be a natural formation expanded by hand.

In the center was an altar, likely for prayer, perhaps even sacrifice, but the room contained little else beyond some shards of pottery. There was no evidence of bones here, and he breathed a relieved sigh—the detonation hadn't damaged anything.

He continued inside. Three openings were ahead. He took the one to the left but could see nothing in the dark, and he wasn't about to risk his neck entering blindly. He checked the second opening with a more direct angle to the outside, the sunlight revealing a stone table with a set of bones lying atop it, shards of cloth still clinging to them, with something sitting atop the ribcage, one hand still clinging to whatever it was.

He tentatively stepped closer, his heart pounding in his ears, his stomach churning as whatever it was the skeleton still gripped after all these years revealed itself.

A wooden cross.

He rushed out onto the ledge and emptied his stomach as he dropped to his knees, his entire body shaking as tears erupted. He had never considered himself a religious man, but to witness what he had just seen, to see the truth of two thousand years shattered in an instant, to throw into question everything two billion people believed, was too much.

He heaved again as he squeezed his eyes shut, his tears turning into sobs as he cried over and over, "I'm so sorry!"

And it wasn't that he blamed himself for making the discovery, it was that he felt for the world and what could become of it.

"What did you find?"

It was Esposito. In his dismay, he hadn't heard the argument below stop, or the man climb the rope. Acton drew several deep, slow breaths, calming himself, then pushed to his feet, wiping his eyes dry on the back of his hands. "Inside, middle opening. He's…He's in there."

Esposito inhaled sharply then rushed inside. A heart-wrenching wail echoed that had Acton's heart breaking once again as a man of true faith had a lifetime of belief torn asunder in a moment. More Keepers climbed onto the ledge then rushed inside, more cries joining in, and Acton simply sat to the side, hugging his knees as he processed what it all meant.

The tablet had been true. They had taken the body of Jesus Christ and entombed him here, faking the resurrection. Someone had recorded the fact for some reason, but whatever that reason was, the truth still remained that the bones were here, and if they were, then it meant the resurrection never took place.

A man who rises from the dead needs his body.

And a man who ascends to Heaven leaves behind no bones.

It was all a crock, perpetrated by eleven friends desperate to continue the teachings of a man they loved.

He closed his eyes and sighed, his breathing steadying. He had to regain control so he could think straight, but the arguments had already begun inside the burial chamber. He couldn't understand what was being said, but the tone was clear.

Rage.

Rage at each other, rage at what it all meant, or just rage at themselves, he had no idea.

But it was rage.

And rage was dangerous.

They were in Syria, one of the most unstable countries in the world, and they needed to be thinking straight if they were to get out of here alive.

Unfortunately, he had the sense everyone here, including himself, had lost the will to live.

West of the Burial Site

South of Homs, Syria

Leather cursed as he peered through the binoculars, half a dozen vehicles heading into the gorge where Acton and the Keepers were located. Four were Syrian, and two were Wagner. He wasn't concerned about the Syrians. They would take prisoners if there was an opportunity, and they likely would only shoot someone if it were a lucky shot.

Wagner, on the other hand, would all be expert shots, and likely were paid a bounty for every enemy they killed. They wouldn't know Acton was there, so wouldn't care that he was worth far more to them alive than dead.

And there were too many of them for his five-man team to engage.

They needed Delta, and even that didn't even the odds numerically, though it did even the odds enough that he'd be willing to put his life at risk in something other than a lost cause.

He activated his comms. "This is Charlie Zero-One. ETA on Bravo Team?"

"Fifteen minutes, Zero-One."

"Copy that. Tell them to come in from the east. We'll cover the west, over."

"Roger that. Relaying now."

"Acknowledged, Zero-One, out."

Leather turned to the others. "It's a suicide mission to go in after them with that many, so let's take those fifteen minutes to get in position so we can have a little surprise party for them. And remember, don't shoot any of the hostage-takers. They'll be on our side for this."

Burial Site

South of Homs, Syria

Several of the Keepers emerged from the cave then climbed over the side, returning to the ground below, and as each one did, the argument died down a little more. Esposito finally emerged, sullen and broken.

"What are your findings, Professor?"

Acton pushed to his feet and sniffed then brushed off his clothes. "I haven't come to any conclusions yet. There is testing that—"

"Your demeanor tells me everything, Professor. You believe that the bones that lie in there belong to Our Lord, Jesus Christ."

The man's voice was barely a whisper, any strength, any pride it once possessed now gone. He was a defeated man, any bravado from earlier conversations surrounding this very possibility beat into submission. It was shocking to see, and it was exactly what Acton had feared should the tablet be true.

Millions, if not billions, would have their faith shaken to the core, and their reaction could be one of sorrow, but it could also be one of rage like he had heard from these true believers only moments before.

Esposito stared at his feet, awaiting an answer, an answer Acton didn't want to give.

"I…I think it's a definite possibility."

Esposito looked up at him. "But you can't be sure?"

"Like I said before, it's impossible to know, but…"

"But?"

"Well, everything on the tablet has proven accurate. Why would anyone go to so much trouble so long ago before a religion was even born to destroy it? If these bones are from that era, and the tablet is as well, then I think it is a distinct possibility, perhaps even likely, that it is indeed Jesus Christ lying in there."

"And if it is, then he is just a man, like you or I."

Acton wasn't sure what to say. "All men are created equal, but not all men are equal. Many waste their lives, some spend their days helping others. If Jesus is the man the Bible describes, then He was a great man with wisdom ahead of His time. If He were just a man like you or I, then would His friends have gone to such trouble? Would billions of people worship Him? There has to be some comfort in that, doesn't there?"

Esposito regarded him for a moment. "I suppose." He drew a deep breath and held it. "There is work to be done."

Acton agreed. "Yes. Let me get in there and start properly documenting things before we move anything. I assume you're going to take the bones with you?"

Esposito shook his head. "No, Professor, like I said before, this could never happen, and it never did."

Acton's eyes narrowed. "What do you mean?"

"I suggest you take one final look. This event will be erased from history very shortly."

Acton tensed. "Wait. Are you going to destroy this place?"

As if to answer his question, a heavy bag was tossed over the ledge followed by the man who had blown the sealing stone. He reached over and more bags were hauled up until finally half a dozen were sitting in front of the cave entrance.

"What's in the bags?"

"Semtex," replied the man.

Acton's eyes shot wide. "Where the hell did you get that?"

"From a greedy Russian."

Acton stepped away from the high explosives. "Don't you think that's a little rash? I mean, we have a piece of history here that should be preserved, not destroyed. If you ever wanted to disprove that they're the bones of Jesus, you'll never be able to if you blow them up."

Esposito pointed to the ropes. "I suggest you get as far away from here as you can."

Acton eyed him. "You mean I'm free to go?"

"Yes."

"And my wife?"

"Was never in any danger. Only I made the threat. She was always safe, no matter what happened here today."

Acton's shoulders slumped in relief. "Thank you." He made one more attempt for reason. "Please, don't do this. At least preserve what we found in the Vault. It will be safe there. It's what you originally planned."

Esposito shook his head. "No. You heard what happened in the cave, even if you didn't understand it. Complete and utter sorrow, anger, hatred, discontent. We could barely come to an agreement on what to do, on what it meant. Imagine what would happen if word were to get out." He took Acton by the arm. "You must never reveal what we found here to anyone. Should the truth get out, our sacrifice will have been for nothing."

Acton eyed him. "Sacrifice? Just what do you have planned?"

Esposito closed his eyes for a moment. "I no longer want to live in a world where Jesus Christ is not the Son of God, nor do the rest of us."

"But that's not what happened here today. We found bones. Yes, they may very well be the bones of Jesus Christ, but they may not be. We can never be certain."

"You don't understand. The fact that men such as us have had our faith shaken to the core makes it true. We can never go back to blind faith. We now have doubt, and that doubt must die with us. A thousand years ago, Romanus understood this. He wanted to know the truth, but died before he could find it. His friend, Alexander, wanted the truth known as well, so left us a message that had to be acted upon. And we did. And now we pay the price knowledge sometimes brings."

Acton grabbed at his hair. "But it's only partial knowledge. All we know is that there are skeletal remains in there. We know nothing else. We are making assumptions that we shouldn't."

"Even you were sick with the discovery."

"Yes. I admit my faith was shaken. It *is* shaken. But let me do my job and figure out what we're dealing with. At least let me take some samples that we can test to determine when this person died."

"No, it will test to the right period, I am sure. This is no hoax. This is the truth. If it weren't, God would have never led us here."

Acton's eyes narrowed. "How do you figure that?"

"He would know the effect this would have on us, yet He led us here regardless. He wanted us to discover the truth, because God is still God, and He wants to put an end to this false religion created by man."

"If God is God, then don't you think he would have put an end to it two thousand years ago?"

An engine roared in the distance and everyone on the ledge turned. Something was shouted from below and Acton's heart leaped into his throat as he spotted what appeared to be a Syrian Army vehicle approaching, with more behind it.

Esposito barked orders and those on the ledge hurriedly hauled the heavy bags of explosives into the tomb as he unslung his assault rifle. "We must delay them until our task is complete."

"Your task, not mine." Acton grabbed the rope then flipped over the side, sliding all the way down before hitting the ground and rolling to absorb the impact. He scrambled over to the truck that had brought him here and took cover behind one of the large tires. "Somebody give me a gun!"

One of the Keepers reached inside and pulled out an AK-47, tossing it to him before scrambling toward the rear of the vehicle. Acton checked the weapon and found a full mag which wouldn't last long in a firefight.

"I need more ammo!"

"Passenger seat floor!"

Acton climbed up into the cabin and found several dozen mags. The Keepers had clearly come prepared for a fight. He stuffed his pockets full, his sense of the situation suggesting he might end up the only one fighting this battle if his former captors were focusing on destroying the tomb.

He dropped back to the ground and took up position, but not before staring up at the eye in the sky he hoped was doing more than just watching.

Anytime now, guys.

West of Burial Site

South of Homs, Syria

Leather sprinted along the hilltop at a crouch, keeping on the opposite side from the gorge where a fight was about to begin. He came to a halt then dropped, crawling to the crest of the hill and peering over. The Syrians and Russians had stopped, turning their vehicles sideways to provide better cover and block off any escape from this end of the gorge. The opposite end was still open and passable, according to Langley, though he had a sense the enemy wasn't concerned about that.

A chopper or drone was a radio call away, and would track any escape.

It was that thought that had him concerned. Langley's latest update was that their entire path back to the border was crawling with Syrian regulars searching for their missing border guards, and the area behind Delta was swarming with Wagner personnel searching for who had slaughtered five of their finest.

Escape would not be by ground, and so far there was no word on any approval for an evac by helicopter. Just like the good old days, where the left hand didn't know what the right foot was doing.

Right now, it was a waiting game. The Syrians below didn't know what they had stumbled upon. In fact, he wasn't even sure. There had been a detonation, but to what end, he couldn't be certain. He assumed they were blowing the entrance to something, and if they were, it meant what was written on the tablet might be true. The idea had him sick to his stomach, which was a bit of a surprise. He hadn't set foot inside a church since he was a child, unless you counted his sham of a wedding. Other than that, there were a few funerals, but nothing else.

He never went voluntarily.

He believed in God, he supposed, but it was never a big part of his life. Yet he still felt sick about what the tablet represented.

There are no atheists in foxholes.

But those questions and answers could wait. Right now, he had a job to do. He had to figure out a way to save his client. He shuffled behind a nearby rock and readied for one hell of a firefight.

A firefight he hoped wouldn't start until Delta arrived.

Someone below opened fire.

Damn.

Acton cursed and pressed against the side panel of the truck as gunfire erupted from overhead. The Keepers on the ledge had fired first, but it only took a moment for the Syrians to return fire. He had a clear view of the ledge overhead, but couldn't see what was happening on it beyond muzzle flashes. If he had to guess, the Keepers were prone, firing from the elevated position. It should provide them with excellent cover, though an RPG or some other grenade could take out the entire lot of them if it found its mark.

Though he doubted they needed much time. All they were doing was delaying until they could get the explosives into position. He wasn't very familiar with high explosives like Semtex, but he knew enough to know that the amount they were stuffing into that small room would not only vaporize the bones, it would collapse the entire hilltop, sealing the tomb forever.

As he held his fire, letting the Syrians concentrate on the Keepers above, he had to admit that what Esposito and the others were doing was probably for the best. Science was one thing, but peace on Earth was something entirely different. It was important to separate the Church from the religion. While the Church might have committed untold horrors in its past, the religion itself was something different. To destroy that faith for the simple pursuit of knowledge wasn't right. Let Esposito obliterate whatever was up there. Preserve the truth known to man. Let things continue as they were.

Whatever the truth that lay above may be.

Bullets pinged off their vehicle as the Syrians returned the fire unwisely initiated by his partner on the ground at the rear of the truck. He was now a target, yet this wasn't his fight. He wasn't certain what to do. Should he try to survive as long as possible? Once the Keepers detonated their explosives, he might escape in the opposite direction in the chaos that would ensue. If the eye in the sky were watching, he could hide in the countryside until they sent in an extraction team.

If he stayed here and engaged the enemy, he would absolutely die.

Decisions, decisions.

Esposito sat on his knees, his hands clasped in front of him as he prayed to God for guidance. The bones of the man who was supposed to be their savior lay before him, undisturbed for two thousand years until today, preserving the lie they had all been taught from youth. The imposter clasped the symbol of their faith in his hands, as if mocking their false convictions, and the embers of hate buried in his stomach glowed in response.

He wanted the false prophet destroyed so no remnant of him could ever be found. He wanted the explosives wired around him to return this filth to the dust from which he had come.

Tears rolled down his cheeks at his thoughts. He was consumed with hatred for the man he had loved only an hour ago. He had been convinced that when they arrived they would find nothing, that the tablet was just an elaborate hoax perpetrated by the Muslims on the unsuspecting Romanus when he captured their city.

He had never dreamed it could be true.

Even Acton's doubts weren't enough to restore his faith. It had been shaken loose, the foundation it had been built upon knocked down, never to be rebuilt. He was prepared to die to preserve this secret, and his only regret was that he would die without the ignorant bliss the rest of the world continued to enjoy.

"Ready!" shouted their explosives guy, Messina, and the gunfire outside quietened as their defenders joined them. They encircled the bones, all bowing their heads, and as Messina counted down from three, Esposito stared one last time at the bones.

And the cross they gripped.

And had a revelation that restored his faith as the blast consumed him.

Acton cursed as the entire hillside erupted above him. He dropped and rolled under the truck as rock sprayed across the gorge. Huge boulders slammed into the ground along with rocks and pebbles, and a thick cloud of pulverized stone rolled over the area, clouding his vision and filling his lungs.

But this was his chance, and he had to be ready. As the debris continued to rain down, he scrambled to the front of the truck and peered into the cloud. Stone was still falling, but the big rocks had to have already landed. He crawled out from under the truck and slung his weapon, then took a leap of faith. He pushed to his feet and sprinted through the cloud, weaving between the rocks that now blocked any escape by vehicle, and covering his head from the small stones still dropping around him.

He didn't bother looking back. Instead, he kept moving forward, kept putting distance between himself and the Syrians, kept heading toward what he hoped was eventual freedom.

When a single shot rang out and he dropped in a heap.

Corpo della Gendarmeria Office

Palazzo del Governatorato, Vatican City

Laura screamed and collapsed into her chair as Giasson rushed forward to stop her from falling to the floor. Everyone in the security office had fallen silent the moment Acton was shot in the back, and all eyes were glued to the screen providing the live feed from Langley.

"Primary is down, I repeat, primary is down."

The voice was calm, almost robotic, the woman providing status updates to the various parties involved emotionless. Yet Giasson could swear he had heard her voice crack. If his understanding of things was accurate, Laura and Acton had worked with the CIA on many occasions, and perhaps there was a bond there between Acton and the automaton on the other end of the speaker.

"Charlie Zero-One, can you confirm status of primary, over?"

"Stand by, Control, we're a little busy here!"

Laura had said the man speaking was her security chief, and Giasson had to admire the fact the man had led a team into Syria to rescue Acton, and was now engaging the enemy despite the man being dead. Most people would have pulled out the moment their client was killed, saving themselves from an enemy that had no clue they were there.

Instead, they were taking their revenge out of loyalty, for Acton wasn't just a client—he was a friend and comrade in arms.

He was their brother.

Part of him wanted to be on the ground, fighting with them. Acton was a good man, one of the best he had the privilege to meet. It was a horrible day. A good man was dead, and from what they could see, the Keepers had blown up an entire hillside to preserve whatever secrets had been inside.

It could mean only one thing

They had found the bones.

The tablet was genuine.

And it made him sick.

He helped Laura onto the couch in his office then turned to Ianuzzi. "Get her some water."

"Yes, sir."

Ianuzzi disappeared and Giasson sat beside the sobbing woman, wrapping an arm around her as the horror story continued to play on the screen in front of them, occasional bursts of gunfire caught on the mics of the brave warriors now battling for their lives.

Please, Lord, take care of these brave men.

He closed his eyes and smiled slightly. Perhaps he hadn't yet completely lost his faith.

Burial Site

South of Homs, Syria

Leather's jaw dropped as Acton hit the ground. He redirected his scope to see who had taken the shot and spotted a Russian looking rather pleased with himself. He put a round in the man's head and he collapsed in a heap. Leather rolled behind the rock as gunfire erupted from below, peppering his position with ricochets. He kept as tight as possible, protecting his head from any strays, cursing himself for having taken the emotional shot.

But he'd do it again in a heartbeat.

Just like a Russian to shoot a man in the back.

He scrambled back down the other side of the hill as the rest of his team engaged, taking some heat off his position. "Target the Russians if you can," he ordered. They were the greater risk, and if he was dying here today, he'd rather take out as many of those bastards here for the money and the violence, rather than the Syrians who were mostly conscripts who'd rather be at home with their families.

Though he'd kill them too if they got in the way.

"Control, ETA on Bravo Team?" he shouted into his comms as he repositioned.

"Five minutes."

"We're not going to be here in five."

"We advise you to fall back, I repeat, fall back. The primary is KIA. Your mission is over. I repeat, your mission is over."

He hit the ground and crawled up to the crest of the hill and checked down below. Acton lay prone, exactly where he had been shot. All evidence said he was dead. Leather peered through his scope, getting a good view of Acton as the firefight continued about twenty yards away.

Where's the blood?

He refocused, squinting slightly. There was no blood on the ground, and he couldn't see a wound on the man's back. It didn't mean there wasn't one, but a round to the back should have produced a rather large pool of blood.

And he could see none.

"Control, Charlie Zero-One. I can't see a wound. I repeat, I can't see a wound on the primary. Stand by." He lined up a shot, slowly exhaling as he squeezed the trigger. A puff of dust exploded just in front of Acton's head.

And Leather could have sworn the man flinched.

A smile spread as Leather rolled onto his back, the Russians opening up on his newly revealed position. But he didn't care. He protected himself once again as he reported the news.

"Control, Charlie Zero-One. The primary is playing possum. I repeat, the primary is playing possum!"

Acton lay on the ground, cursing himself for having reacted to the stray shot that had missed his head by only a couple of feet. It must have been a ricochet, since there was no way the Syrians could have made that shot without hitting him.

Unless it came from an elevated position.

If his enemy was now spreading along the hilltops, his playing Weekend at Bernie's would soon be over. When he had been shot, it had knocked the wind right out of him and his ass to the ground. As near as he could figure, the round had hit his rifle slung across his back. His weapon was probably useless now, but it had saved his life.

The heavy gunfire behind him changed pitch once again as at least some of the guns redirected toward a new target that still wasn't him. His playing dead was so far working, but he wasn't sure what to do now. Would the Syrians be paying attention to him still, or were they engaged with whoever it was now fighting them?

And that was the real question. Who were they fighting? It could be some rival faction, though he had a feeling it wasn't. It had to be Delta, yet the weapons didn't sound right. He was hearing C8 Carbines instead of M4s. Whoever it was, if it was an enemy of my enemy is my friend situation, then he should take advantage of it while he could. Whoever won in the end would still be his enemy, and he'd be at their mercy.

And if it were Delta, or some other friendly, the best way to help them was to haul ass out of here so they could disengage.

He spotted a large stone ahead, one that appeared to have been freshly deposited from the explosion, and inhaled deeply, steadying his nerves.

Here goes nothing.

He rose and sprinted toward the rock, diving behind it then pressing his back against it.

And not a shot was fired in his direction.

Okay, this might just work.

He picked his next target and readied himself.

Acton/Palmer Residence

St. Paul, Maryland

Reading winced as Mai hugged him hard, his wounds protesting angrily. But he didn't care. The horror of a moment ago had been replaced by jubilation in the room. Tommy was jumping up and down, fist-pumping his relief, as Mai wiped fresh tears of joy after so many of pain.

And his poor heart slowly eased back on the hammering as relief set in.

His friend was alive.

And being an idiot once again.

They all stared at the screen, the live feed provided by Langley welcome but horrifying, especially the bits of comms traffic. Right now, he was focused on what Acton was doing. He was alive and sprinting from one large rock to another, pushing his luck each time as he attempted to put some distance between himself and the fighting.

Reading could understand the motivation. While Leather's team was taking on the enemy, why not take advantage of the distraction and make

259

your escape? But his friend had already somehow cheated death once. Tempting fate twice seemed unwise.

Though would he have done anything differently?

Reading was just thankful his friend hadn't joined in the firefight and drawn even more attention to himself. For the moment, Leather's team of five were keeping the Syrians and Russians preoccupied, but he could tell things were about to take a turn for the worse.

The Wagner mercenaries were regrouping and directing their Syrian counterparts as heavier weaponry was retrieved from their vehicles. This battle would soon be over if Delta didn't get there soon, and even then, they were only six.

He might yet lose his friend today.

Burial Site

South of Homs, Syria

Acton crouched behind another large rock, one of the last that lay ahead of him. He had already cleared the majority of the debris field left behind by the Keepers' explosion that destroyed all the evidence of why they were here and allowed his captors a sinful exit from the world created by their troubling discovery.

Such a waste.

The moral debate over what they had done, however, would have to wait for another time. He had to figure out a way out of here that didn't leave him horribly exposed. If he crawled the rest of the way, he would remain out of sight, but with the distance left to cover, the fight behind him could be long over before he could clear the gorge. As well, he had to think of whoever was behind him, fighting his enemies for him. It had to be Delta, and the sooner he was safely out of here, the sooner they could withdraw.

261

He rose to a knee, ready to do a poor imitation of Usain Bolt when a series of odd popping sounds were followed by several strange reports that echoed through the gorge. An explosion erupted behind him and he spun as two more blasts tore through the area. The vehicles the enemy had arrived in burst into fireballs, screams from some of the troops sending a shiver down his spine as the entire gorge filled with a white smoke that had nothing to do with the fires now raging.

"Friendlies on your six!" came a voice from behind that he recognized as Dawson's. He spun again to see half a dozen men in desert gear rushing toward him, M4s raised, Dawson in the lead. The instantly recognizable Atlas was carrying some beast of a weapon slung over his shoulder that Acton suspected was what had taken out the vehicles. Dawson pointed at him and Niner rushed forward, dropping to a knee.

"Man, am I happy to see you guys." Acton's eyes narrowed. "Wait, if you're here, who's back there?"

"Leather and his team." Niner spun him around and checked his back. He whistled. "Doc, you are one lucky sonofabitch. Not a scratch. But you're going to have one hell of a bruise. When the adrenaline wears off, you're going to be in for a world of hurt for a few days."

"I can live with that." Gunfire erupted from Bravo Team and Acton jerked a thumb over his shoulder. "Go join your buddies. I'll be fine."

Niner slapped him on the shoulder then turned his back to him, showing him his backpack. "Main pouch. Body armor." Acton opened the backpack and pulled out the armor, immediately donning it and tightening it up. Niner pointed in the direction they had arrived from.

"Head that way. You'll find our SUV at the far end. It's up-armored. Get inside, stay low."

Acton shook his head. "Give me a weapon. I can help."

"Bullshit. We're here to save your ass. If you get killed, then we'll have wasted a perfectly good day, and I swear I'll marry your wife. Get the hell out of here, Doc."

Acton chuckled then smacked the warrior on the shoulder. "Thanks, buddy." He scrambled back to his feet and sprinted toward the far end of the gorge as his friends continued to engage, and he said a silent prayer to both God and Jesus Christ for their safety, wondering if one was a wasted effort.

Dawson slipped his gasmask in place as he and the others continued forward through the mix of smoke grenades and tear gas. The enemy was coughing and gasping for breath as his men on the ground and Leather's from the hilltops eliminated the struggling hostiles. It was now a turkey shoot. He had no problem killing any of these men. The Russians were vermin, and the Syrians little better—he had no doubt they had violated plenty of human rights during their stints serving their country.

The detonations from the Gustaf's several rounds had done a lot of their work for them, taking out over half the hostiles according to his update from Langley as they had entered the fray. The confusion that ensued had allowed Leather's team to fire freely, and Bravo Team merely mopped up what was left.

Fast and effective.

Just the way he liked it.

"Hold your fire!" he ordered as it became clear the only weapons firing were friendly. The guns fell silent as the breeze channeling through the gorge cleared out the smoke and tear gas. He slung his M4 and drew his Glock, carefully stepping through the carnage. Some of the enemy could still be alive and stupid enough to make a last stand. He had no intention of executing anyone, but he would remove them from this world should they pose a threat.

Something moved to his left and Atlas fired, putting two rounds in the head of a Wagner scumbag as he reached for his weapon beside him.

Definitely no tears shed for him.

They finished clearing the area and Dawson held up a hand. "All clear!" He peered up at the hilltops and saw Leather and his men emerge on either side, waving down at them.

"It's about time you showed up," called Leather with a smile.

Dawson shrugged. "I figured you could handle things yourselves. Was I wrong?"

"Naw, we just needed a few more minutes."

"Zero-One, Control. We've got multiple enemy units headed your way. It looks like your firefight caught their attention or they got a call out. Either way, the forward elements will reach you within five minutes, over."

Dawson cursed. "Which end of the gorge will they arrive at first?"

"East end where you came in from."

Another curse. "ETA on our evac?"

"Ten minutes."

Yet another curse. "Understood. Have them land at the west end of the gorge and tell them to hurry the hell up."

"Copy that, Zero-One. Control, out."

Dawson turned to Niner. "Go get the Doc. We've got more shit headed our way, and they'll be reaching him first."

Niner gave a two-fingered salute then shrugged out of his backpack before sprinting in the direction he had sent Acton only minutes before.

Dawson waved up to Leather. "Hold your positions! We've got hostiles coming in from both directions. First arriving at the east end, ETA five minutes. This isn't over yet."

Leather gave him a thumbs-up then disappeared along with the others on the high ground.

"Spock, rig some boobytraps in this wreckage. I want anyone coming through here on foot wishing they hadn't. We're going to go set up a welcoming committee at the west end of the gorge. You hang back and make sure your handiwork doesn't take out the Doc and Niner."

"You got it, BD."

Dawson waved a hand at the others. "Let's get a move on, gentlemen. We've got an LZ to secure."

Acton spotted the SUV and breathed a relieved sigh as he slammed against it, gasping for breath. Niner had been right. He had been running on adrenaline, and now that it was clearing his system, the pain was setting in. He had a feeling he had some bruised ribs, perhaps from the fall, and his breathing was slightly labored. If he were at Home Depot, he wouldn't be concerned, but he was in Syria less than a mile from intense fighting.

The pounding in his ears slowly settled and he noticed the gunfire had stopped. He had to assume the good guys had won after what he had seen upon Bravo Team's arrival. They were exceptional, and it showed what excellent training and the right firepower could do even when outnumbered. They had walked in, fired some sort of anti-tank weapon a few times, lobbed in smoke and tear gas, then gone to town.

He'd be surprised if the entire battle had lasted more than five minutes.

He climbed into the driver's seat and found the keys in the visor. He fired up the engine and cranked the air conditioning, enjoying the cool air as it wafted over him. The body armor was uncomfortable and hot, but it could save his life should something go wrong. He had learned long ago to never assume things were over just because the gunfire had stopped.

He took the opportunity to give the cabin a once over, and found spare comms gear sitting in the console. He fit it in place and gulped.

"—three minutes. You need to get the primary out of there before they arrive."

"This is One-One. I'm on it. I can only run so damned fast."

Acton recognized Niner's voice. The questions were, who was the primary, and who was arriving? He activated the comms. "This is Acton. I found a spare set of comms."

"Professor, this is Control. We need you to get back to the others ASAP. You've got hostiles arriving in less than three minutes. Do you copy?"

Acton put the SUV in gear and hammered on the gas, sending him surging toward the battle he had just fled. "I copy. I'm in their SUV. I'm driving toward them now. I'm not sure how far I can get, but I'll switch to foot when I have to."

"Copy that, Professor. One-One is on his way to you on foot."

"Copy that. Tell him I'll be there shortly."

"I hear ya, Doc. Don't worry about babying her. This is one rental I'm happy we took the insurance out on."

Acton smiled as he guided the SUV through the rock-strewn gorge floor. It was wide enough for him to make his way around the larger stones, but as he got deeper in, he scraped the hell out of the paint job.

And it was kind of fun.

He spotted Niner flagging him down ahead. He pulled up beside the man and Niner climbed in. "Hiya, Doc. No time for hugs and kisses. Let's get the hell out of here."

"Primary has picked up One-One," came the report in his ear for the benefit of the others.

Acton continued forward, picking his way through, when gunfire erupted from behind them, several rounds pinging off the reinforced SUV's body. He cursed and instinctively ducked, his foot easing off the accelerator.

"Punch it, Doc! And sit up. If they hit us with anything big enough to make it through, you're dead anyway."

267

Acton wasn't sure he liked the sound of that. In fact, he was quite sure he didn't, but he hammered on the gas as he sat up, getting a better view of the path ahead. He glanced in the rearview mirror and spotted a light utility vehicle pursuing them, two men standing in the rear firing at them with assault rifles.

Sometimes he hated when he was right.

Never assume things were over just because the gunfire had stopped.

Leather lay prone on the hilltop as he peered through his scope toward the far end of the gorge. Acton's SUV was weaving between larger and larger boulders, and was about to reach the main debris field from the earlier explosion that had taken out a significant portion of the hillside.

It was impassible.

It meant Acton and Niner would have to get out and cover the rest of the way on foot, making them sitting ducks. At the moment, they were being pursued by only one vehicle, though apparently more were already arriving at the far end. There was no time for them to wait in the car. This had to end now.

He took careful aim then squeezed the trigger. The pursuing driver slumped then the vehicle swerved, riding up the hillside before tipping over, spilling out its occupants. More shots rang out from the other members of his team, and the survivors dropped, the threat eliminated.

"Bravo One-One, Charlie Zero-One. You're all clear behind you, over."

"Copy that, Zero-One. Thanks for the assist."

The SUV slowed, the panic gone for the moment, and Leather watched as it reached the blocked debris field and came to a halt. Acton and Niner climbed out and jogged toward Spock's position.

"This is Control. Hostiles are arriving at the west end now. Prepare to engage."

Leather cursed. This wasn't over yet.

Dawson took up position as Atlas fired his third and final round at the oncoming Syrians, two vehicles already aflame, and now a third, every one of the big man's shots true. This had the enemy scrambling. Atlas had taken out troop transports, maximizing the casualties, though it appeared they were still facing about twenty with more on the way and no more rounds for the Gustaf.

Where the hell is our air support?

If this lasted much longer, they'd be overwhelmed from all sides.

"Conserve your ammo!" he ordered. "Make every shot count. We don't know how long we're going to be stuck here. Let's just keep them back for as long as we can."

A string of acknowledgments from the others was followed by a cessation of the suppression fire. This had the Syrians tentatively standing to see what was going on.

"Hold your fire. Let's see how stupid they get."

All fire ceased from their position and Dawson watched as more of the Syrians rose. Some still wisely hid behind their vehicles, recognizing that they couldn't have won the battle with barely a shot fired from their side, but there was the possibility his team had left.

He counted ten.

"Watch your arcs. Open fire." He squeezed his trigger, taking out his first target, immediately moving on to the next one without waiting to see if he had hit the first. Atlas, Jimmy, and Jagger did the same, and within moments they were facing half what they had been.

Let's go, Navy!

Acton reached Spock who held out a hand, stopping them just ahead of the carnage from earlier. His chest ached and he gasped for breath, and he wasn't sure how much longer he could keep up this pace.

"Good to see you, Doc. You okay?"

"Bruised ribs, I think. Just having a hard time getting deep breaths. Every one of them hurts."

Niner frowned. "I'll check you out when I get the chance, Doc, but you're just going to have to suck it up for now. If all goes to plan, we're out of here any minute now."

Gunfire from either end of the gorge suggested otherwise.

They turned to see two vehicles approaching from the east, and three sets of curses erupted. Spock pointed the way. "Follow me exactly. I've boobytrapped the area to make them think twice. Let's not get ourselves killed now, shall we?"

Acton picked his way through the wreckage, following Spock's footsteps precisely, his heart pounding with every tripwire pointed out. They were through in an eternity that lasted less than a minute, then were sprinting once again toward the lesser of two evils.

The gunfight at the west end.

270

Rather than the fresh arrivals from the east.

I just want to go home.

Corpo della Gendarmeria Office

Palazzo del Governatorato, Vatican City

Laura's pulse pounded as she watched everything unfolding from overhead. To the right of the screen, she could see James with two others the voice from Langley had identified as Niner and Spock. They were running toward the others as two loads of soldiers emptied out of transports that had just arrived from the east end of the gorge.

They were hopelessly outnumbered.

She bit her finger as muzzle flashes erupted from the new arrivals, then cheered with the others in Giasson's now crowded office as Leather's team opened up from their elevated position, taking down a large number of the new arrivals, sending them into disarray. James and the others continued their escape as Leather engaged, and within minutes James had joined Dawson and the others, and the Syrians from the east were retreating on foot.

She buried her face in her hands as her shoulders shook, her sobs a mix of terror and relief. She wasn't sure how much more of this her poor heart could take, and the thought had her wondering how Reading and his genuinely poor heart was doing.

"Additional hostiles arriving from the north, ETA sixty seconds."

"This is ridiculous!" cried someone. "Why don't they get them out of there?"

She had been asking herself the same question repeatedly, but knew from experience it took time for air assets to get into position. They couldn't have been deployed until they knew the status, and this battle had begun barely fifteen minutes ago. Even the fastest aircraft took time.

"What are those?" asked Giasson, sitting beside her as he pointed at the left of the screen, four dark shapes entering the bird's eye view from the west.

Laura wiped her eyes clear then smiled.

"Helicopters!"

West of Burial Site

South of Homs, Syria

Dawson looked up as four Bell AH-1W SuperCobra attack helicopters blew past them, their weapons pods lighting up as scores of rockets launched, streaking toward the enemy positions. Explosion after explosion erupted and he and the others rose to watch the beautiful sight.

Shock and awe on a small scale.

The entire show took less than two minutes, and soon Control was in his ear reporting the general retreat taking place. But their reprieve might not last long. The Syrians could have air power of their own in the area within minutes. When the Osprey arrived, they would have to be quick about it.

He activated his comms. "Charlie Zero-One, this is Bravo Zero-One. Get your team to the LZ ASAP, over."

"Roger that, Zero-One. On our way," responded Leather.

Dawson turned to see Acton gasping for breath, something he shouldn't be doing. Niner was examining him, concern on his face. Dawson joined them. "Status?"

"He's having some trouble breathing. Might be some bruised or cracked ribs."

Acton dismissed their concerns with a wave of his hand. "I'll be okay. It's just all the running. I can't get a full breath without it hurting, so I'm just winded. I'll settle down soon enough."

"Understood. Niner, you're responsible for him. Get him on the Osprey the moment it touches down."

"You got it."

Dawson peered in the distance, the distinctive sound of the Osprey's rotors now within earshot. He did a quick mental tally of his men and Leather's as they arrived, confirming what he already knew. No casualties, no wounded except possibly Acton. The man should be dead, though, so some temporary breathing issues were nothing to be worried about.

His men popped smoke to not only mark their position but to obscure the evac from any hostiles that might have hung around, though he doubted there were any in fighting shape, the SuperCobras having done their job swiftly and effectively.

He cleared the LZ and took a knee as the Osprey touched down, its tilt rotors something he'd never get tired of seeing. And as he waved his men on board, he wondered just what the hell Acton had found back there, and whether it meant all his time spent in church had been wasted.

He prayed not.

Kınalıada Island, Eastern Roman Empire

AD 1072

Alexander stood on the shore, awaiting the arrival of his best friend whom he hadn't seen in over a year. Romanus had been forbidden visitors and any contact with his former allies, of which Alexander was considered one of the closest. Yet for some reason, he had been granted permission to see his old friend, his old emperor. In fact, he hadn't requested the meeting. He had never requested one the entire time, for he was well aware of the conditions of the agreement. Instead, he had received a message from Emperor Michael himself granting him permission to see Romanus on this day at this location.

He was eager to see his friend. It had been too long, and this might be the last time they saw each other, or perhaps the first of many should some leniency now be shown toward a man who was never a threat to the emperor or the Doukai family—once Romanus gave his word, it was absolute.

276

"Here they come," said one of the monks standing nearby. Little had been said upon his arrival beyond him presenting the documentation allowing him to be there, then being told where to stand. He had a sense they knew something about what was happening, though he couldn't be sure. After all, these were monks, unaccustomed to interacting with the high society of Constantinople, and certainly had little experience in hosting a former emperor.

He spotted the boat pulling through the morning fog, the sail drawn down as the tiller steered them to the dock. Several men jumped from the small boat onto the dock as monks rushed forward to assist, and soon they were tied off. Alexander stepped forward as a hooded figure was helped from the boat.

"Romanus, is that you, my friend?" he asked tentatively, uncertain, for the man in front of him was broken, a shadow of the mighty warrior he had called friend for decades.

"Alexander?" The voice was weak, hoarse, all the pride it once held now gone.

"Yes, it's me."

A withered hand reached out and he took it, shocked at how emaciated it was. "It is you, isn't it?"

"It is."

Romanus cried out and collapsed into his arms, his shoulders shaking as he wept. "Forgive me, my friend, for I have no more honor left in me. They have broken me, and my only wish is to die." His friend grabbed him by the shoulder and looked up at him, the hood that covered his face slipping down his neck, giving Alexander his first glimpse of his old friend.

And he recoiled in horror.

Romanus' eyes were no more, his face caked in blood, maggots wriggling in the sockets that once contained his piercing eyes. It was the most horrifying thing he had ever seen. Nothing on the battlefield compared to this, for this was a living man, and this man was his friend.

"Who did this to you?"

"John. John Doukas."

"That bastard! He shall pay for this!"

Romanus pressed his forehead against Alexander's chest. "You must do me one last favor, my friend."

"Anything."

"Kill me." The demand was gasped out, a desperate cry from a tortured man who had lost all hope. Alexander could only imagine how horrendous the pain must be, and as much as it sickened him, he had no choice.

He must honor his friend's wish.

"You have my word." He paused. "But first, there is a matter we must discuss."

"Make it brief, my friend, for I wish to be free of this hell as quickly as possible."

Alexander turned to the others. "A chair!"

One was tossed from the boat and positioned nearby. He helped Romanus onto it then kneeled in front of him. He lowered his voice. "I have brought the tablet with me."

Romanus stared at him through dead eyes, and it was everything Alexander could do to not gag. "You must find the truth. I failed, so now it is your duty."

"But with you no longer our emperor, there is no hope of getting to the location indicated on the tablet."

"You must try. And if not you, then some future you. Your son, your grandson. The truth must be determined. Promise me you will try."

Alexander squeezed his eyes shut as Romanus reached out, pressing his palm against Alexander's chest. Alexander clasped it. "You have my word that someday, someone will determine the truth. But I am afraid, my friend, that you will know the truth long before I."

Romanus smiled, patting him on the chest. "I think you may be right, old friend." He inhaled deeply and squared his shoulders. "Now do it."

"Forgive me, my emperor." Alexander stood and drew his sword, swinging it in a wide arc, decapitating his friend in a single stroke. Everyone around him stood in stunned silence, uncertain as to what to do. Alexander sheathed his sword then reached out, gently lowering his friend's body to the dock before he fell from the chair.

Somebody shouted in the background, what, Alexander didn't care, for he wept like he never had in his life. His best friend was dead, and he had delivered the final blow. He said a silent prayer for the soul of the greatest man he had ever known, then stood as the boat pushed away from the dock, the crew desperate to flee the scene.

He turned to the abbot, who stood nearby, his mouth agape. "You will see to his burial, with full honors, of course."

The man tore his eyes from the sight. "Y-yes. Of course."

"Good." Alexander patted the satchel slung over his shoulder, the tablet heavier now than only moments before. "I have something here that must be buried with him."

"I understand."

Alexander stared down at his friend's head, and squeezed his eyes shut.

I'm sorry, my friend, but it will be up to some future soul to determine the truth, not I, nor my descendants.

Corpo della Gendarmeria Office

Palazzo del Governatorato, Vatican City

Present Day

Acton sat in Giasson's office, gently taking deep breaths as his ribs, or more accurately, rib, continued to knit. X-rays on the USS Iwo Jima had revealed a single cracked rib and no other collateral damage. He would be fine in a couple of weeks, though sore, especially for the next few days.

The evac had been somber for him, as it had finally given him some time to process what had happened with the Keepers and the tomb. There was no way to be certain what they had found, and now that the entire location had been destroyed, the truth could never be known. Pressed by Bravo Team and Leather, all he had managed to tell them was that he didn't know what he had found, but he had found something.

Just talking was difficult, so it had saved him from any further explanation.

"It's here."

They all looked up as Ianuzzi whispered the message from the doorway.

'It' could be only one thing.

"When did it arrive?" asked Giasson.

"Just a few minutes ago. Private courier to his Holiness' office, marked for his eyes only."

"And?"

"His assistant opened it under our supervision. It is the tablet."

"Any message?" asked Laura.

"Just a single page with their symbol, and the words, 'For the Vault.' printed below it."

Acton sighed. "And another piece of history gets buried for eternity."

Giasson shrugged. "What would you have us do? If what you say is true, think of the trouble it could cause."

Laura tapped her chin. "You know, I've been thinking about what you said. You said you found the bones, as the tablet said, but what made you think it was, you know, *Him*?"

Acton closed his eyes, picturing the scene, something he would never forget for the rest of his life. "He was gripping a wooden cross on his chest."

Laura's eyebrows rose. "Wait. A wooden cross?"

"Yes."

She smiled then leaped to her feet, facing everyone. "It's not Him!"

They stared at her, puzzled.

"What do you mean?" asked Acton.

"Think about it. Jesus is crucified on the cross. He's entombed. Whoever wrote the tablet then unseals the tomb, steals the body, then hides it to the north where you found it. Why does he put a cross on the body, only days after His death?"

"So there's no doubt who it is?" suggested Giasson.

She jabbed a finger at him. "Exactly!"

Acton shook his head. "I'm sorry, hon, but you'll have to explain it to us. We're not getting it."

She grinned. "The cross is a symbol of Christ and Christianity. It didn't become that symbol until centuries later. There is absolutely no possible way someone from His era would have known to put it there as a symbol of who He was!"

Acton's jaw dropped, stunned that he had missed that fact. She was right. The cross was never a symbol of Jesus until centuries after he died. He leaped to his feet as his faith was rapidly restored. "That means the body was from at least the fourth century, and more likely, it was from the eleventh! Whoever forged the tablet that Romanus found probably created it for him, and took an old body from another tomb and sealed it where we found it in order to trick Romanus into thinking everything he believed and fought for was a fraud. Whoever did this was trying to destroy the Christian faith, and sow disarray among the Byzantines."

Giasson collapsed into his chair, relief on his face. "And they very nearly succeeded a thousand years later."

Acton sat and Laura joined him, clasping his hand, smiles dominating the room. It had all been a hoax, an elaborate one from a thousand years ago, and he had fallen for it. They all had. He had been so blinded by the

283

shock of finding a body, that the significance of the cross, so obviously out of place now, had been lost on him.

He closed his eyes and said a silent prayer, begging for forgiveness.

And for the Good Lord to have mercy on the souls of the Keepers of the One Truth who had gone to their grave believing his misinterpretation of what they had found.

Lord, please forgive me.

THE END

ACKNOWLEDGMENTS

This book almost killed me. Literally. A week before the deadline, stressed to the nines, I had a bit of an anxiety attack as I am sometimes prone to do with all my health issues, and my heart rate shot up to 125, leading to my lungs filling with fluid.

As I coughed, struggling to clear the buildup for the next hour, my blood oxygen stats collapsed to the mid-fifties, then slowly recovered into the sixties then seventies, but were still dangerously low. Barely able to talk, I sent a text to my daughter, who of course was asleep at that hour. I called her and she thankfully answered, and I gasped for her to check her texts. I sent the details and she was there within thirty minutes.

The next two hours were spent with me continuing to battle breathing, but my O2 continued to slowly improve, until it was bouncing between the mid-seventies and mid-eighties, but never reaching the normal of 95% or higher. I knew I wasn't getting better quickly enough, and the few times in the past something similar had happened, it had completely cleared up in an hour.

This was something different.

My daughter called 9-1-1 and an ambulance was dispatched around 4am. She packed me a bag, gathered my electronics, chargers, meds, water, snacks, and various other sundries, then let the paramedics in, answering their questions when I couldn't.

I was put on oxygen then taken to the hospital, and because there were concerns it was my heart, I was in a bed within about half an hour, then sent for chest X-rays. Blood was taken and I continued to improve over the hours. The X-ray showed possible pneumonia, though I knew that was wrong since I still practice strict Covid protocols because of my health problems.

I was discharged later that afternoon and a friend picked me up and drove me home. The first day home was just sleeping pretty much through until almost midday the following day. Easter dinner was canceled, but I felt much better. As I'm writing this, I'm still exhausted, and am still recovering, but am confident I'll be fine in short order.

All of this, of course, affected finishing this book, and it was once again down to the wire.

My daughter was a trooper through this entire thing, and I love her so much for it. I don't know what I would have done if it weren't for her. It brings tears to my eyes just typing this as I think of how scared she must have been seeing her father gasping for breath for hours before being taken away in an ambulance.

I'm so sorry for what I put you through, Niskha.

So what had me under so much stress? The deadline. The history on this took a lot longer to write than planned, because so much of it actually happened. Usually when I write the "history" portion of an Acton, it is either completely made up, or it takes one small piece of history then expands upon it. In this case, all the players except Alexander actually existed, Romanus' story from the failed coup attempt to the marriage to the victories, defeats, betrayals, torture, and death (though not the method), all happened. To be faithful to the history and timelines involved took time, time I didn't have.

In the end, I got it done, but I think I'm going to take a breather. Check the release date of this book and the next one in my bibliography to see whether I kept that promise to myself.

As usual, there are people to thank. My dad for all the research, Ian Kennedy for some explosives info, and, as always, my wife, my daughter, my late mother who will always be an angel on my shoulder as I write, as well as my friends for their continued support, and my fantastic proofreading team!

To those who have not already done so, please visit my website at www.jrobertkennedy.com, then sign up for the Insider's Club to be notified of new book releases. Your email address will never be shared or sold.

Thank you once again for reading.